"SOMETIMES THE GUILTY ARE THE
ONES WE LEAST EXPECT"
– DAVIDA BALDWIN

THE UNUSUAL SUSPECTS

A NOVEL BY TIONA DAWKINS

PUBLISHER'S NOTE:
This book is a work of fiction. Names, characters, businesses,
Organizations, places, events and incidents are the product of the
Author's imagination or are used fictionally. Any resemblance of
Actual persons, living or dead, events, or locales are entirely coin-
cidental.

Library of Congress Control Number: 2010922223
ISBN: 0-9823913-3-1
ISBN 13: 978-0-9823913-3-4
Cover Design: Davida Baldwin www.oddballdsgn.com
Editor: Advanced Editorial Services
Graphics: Davida Baldwin
www.thecartelpublications.com
First Edition

Printed in the United States of America

ACKNOWLEDGEMENTS

I would first like to thank T. Styles, Charisse Washington and the whole Cartel staff for giving me and so many other first time authors an opportunity to see our dreams come true. Thanks for believing in me and this story. I love y'all.

To Niccole Simmons at 21st Street Urban Editing, thank you so much for being so thorough and taking the time to make this novel read like we envisioned. Thanks for believing in me the way that you do. I won't let you or The Cartel down.

To my sister Keisha: Since we were children I've always wanted to be just like you. As we became women, that still holds true. I am so angry and hurt that I have to go through this thing called life without you. Keisha, I feel lost and empty. One whole half of me is missing; however, I'm so grateful that God allowed us the time he did.

Sister your strength amazes me. You are truly my hero for all that you endured to stay with us. It's because of you that I will fear nothing in this world. It gives me much comfort knowing you're no longer in pain and as much as it hurts I know we must let you finally rest. I know how much you wanted to be able to just hold this book in your hands and I apologize that you didn't get the opportunity to do so. Just know that every word I write will be with the hopes of keeping you proud.

I love you and there is no way to explain how much I'll miss you, my sister. So until you meet me at the gate, I'll see you in my dreams. You're forever in my heart, soul and spirit. Rest In Peace; and enjoy heaven, for you truly deserve it.

Your baby sis,

What's Up Fam,

Thank you for continuing to come back. We appreciate the love and loyalty you continue to show.

"The Unusual Suspects" is a heavy hitter. It's a little different from our previous releases as it's geared toward our younger readers, but it's still packed wit' Cartel Power, so enjoy it!

Now for an update, the Cartel Publications family is happy to announce that this summer, our very own Eyone Williams, author of "Hell Razor Honeys", will be coming home. He is being released on parole in May, just in time for his new banger, "Hell Razor Honeys 2". We will be throwing him a huge welcome home/book release party at the Cartel Café' & Books store in Oxon Hill, MD so be on the lookout for the date announcement. If you've ever been to any of our parties, you know we gets it in, hope to see you there!

As a Cartel Publications tradition, we pay homage to a vet or new kid in the literary game making their mark. In this novel we are proud to pay our respects to:

"Sister Souljah"

Sister Souljah is a world famous author, activist and film producer who has dedicated her time and passion to African American history. Although her first novel, "No Disrespect" dropped in 1995, she is best known for her street lit classic, "The Coldest Winter Ever" which was published in 1999 but is still selling strong today. Her latest, "Midnight: A Gangster Love Story" was also an instant hit from the moment it dropped. The Cartel Publications respects the work Sister Souljah has put in and continues to put down.

Aight Fam, ya'll get to it! Don't forget to follow us on Twitter and Facebook or stop by our store in Oxon Hill, MD. The address is 5011 B Indian Head Hwy. Oxon Hill, MD 20745. Call 240/ 724-7225 for more information.

Be Easy!
Charisse "C. Wash" Washington
VP, The Cartel Publications
www.thecartelpublications.com
www.twitter.com/cartelbooks
www.facebook.com/thecartelpublications
www.facebook.com/cartelcafeandbooks

FEBRUARY 28, 2010

" *T*oday in the news, our top story, what some are calling the most anticipated trial of the year is set to begin this morning. We have Linda Blackwood, reporting from the courthouse."

"It all began eight months ago, when the FBI announced that after a long two year investigation, three women were indicted on multiple charges of fraud, drug trafficking and murder. Some incidents date back to crimes committed over seven years ago.

Federal prosecutors say Jada Cruz, twenty-six, Solace Ford, also age twenty-six and twenty-five year old Angel Washington, all of Pennsylvania, are responsible for more than ten unsolved murders and disappearances in the last six years. Prosecutors say the trio is also the head of one of the country's largest drug operations. If convicted, they all face life behind bars, without the possibility of parole. I'm Linda Blackwood, reporting live from the downtown Philadelphia court house, back to you at the studio Rob and Sandy."

••

"Hot 97", where hip-hop and R & B lives. You got the morning show, live on ya radio, it's ya girl Ms. Jones on Hot 97 in the morning with Michael Shawn and Envy. It's 7:53a.m. y'all, so if you have to be to work by eight, you need to blow ya horns real loud at the A- hole stalling at the lights.

Yeah; and if you on the highway cut a few people off, give 'em the finger or whatever you need to do to get there on time."

"See, you stupid fa dat, you always gotta take it too far, Envy."

Anyway, we just finished the phone jack with Carmen, if you missed it you can hear it again at eight fifty am. But right now, we goooottaaa talk about these chicks from Philly dats on trial for evvvveryything. Nah, fa real. How they gonna bring up stuff that happened seven years ago? Ain't it a law or suttin' against that? If not, we need to be fightin' for one. If you ain't catch 'em within three years, then oh well, you suck as a detective and you can't indict after dat."

"You know what, Jonesy? I'm wit' dat."

"Yeah, I bet! Anyway, they sayin' these chicks were like the Queen Pins of Philly. Everything movin' was comin' from them. Everywhere, too. Rhode Island, Connecticut, Massachusetts, N.Y, Jersey, Delaware, Maryland, Virginia, D C..."

"This list is crazy."

"Yeah, they fine as hell too. I don't know, but it's something sexy about a female gangster. Callin' the shots and pushin' all that weight. Have you seen their pictures, Michael Shawn?"

"Yeah, Envy, I seen 'em. That chick Jada could be my third baby mutha, fa real."

"Y'all stuuupid. Only y'all would be thinking like dat. They fine, but they still some murderers."

"Allegedly, Jonesy. Allegedly."

"Yeah, you right on that one, Envy. Allegedly, cuz we don't need any more drama up at Hot 97. No more lawsuits."

"The trial supposed to be on Tru T V. I set my DVR to record it every day. I'ma go home, turn it on, get my Vaseline and ummm."

"Ilk! I believe you too, Michael Shawn."

"They too fine to go to jail, I hope they get off," said Envy.

"I don't know. They were gettin' it. They should of been on the remix wit' Fifty, Diddy, and Jay." Jonesy said laughingly.

"You ever see them on TV? They are fine as hell!"

"Michael Shawn...."

"Na, girl, I'm serious. That girl Jada, baby girl is about five-eight, honey brown eyes, long beautiful curly hair. My boy told me she drives a Diamond White Aston Martin with all white cashmere leather interior and eighteen-inch chrome wheels. Then you got o'girl Lace, she's short about five-three, one forty, Puerto Rican and black, high yellow complexion. She has chinky eyes long curly pretty braids. She drives a silver Rolls Royce Phantom, grey and white interior, chrome wheels and last but not least you got Angel, and she is light brown complexion, about five-five, one-thirty to one-forty, medium length sandy brown hair with blond highlights, she wears it in a cute bobbed cut. Man, them girl's ain't nothing nice. Angel drives a candy red Mercedes Benz SLR convertible on some chrome dubs."

The station was quiet for a brief second. "Uh, don't you think you know a little too much about them? I mean...their body types and their cars too, Michael Shawn?"

"Jonesy, there are two things I know. Women and cars, way before those girls got caught up, people were talking about their cars. They always had the flyest whips around."

"We should have someone who knows them on the show," Jonesy continued. "If you a friend or relative of one of the chicks on trial and you wanna call in and shed some light on this thing for us wit' out incriminating ya-self, give us a call."

"Yeah, call in, especially if they happen to call you collect from jail. I wanna get on Jada's visiting list."

"Seeeee, seeee...always takin' stuff too far, Michael Shawn. Right now let's get into the new Melanie Fiona, 'It Kills Me', I love this song!"

"And it kills meee, to know how much I really love youuu.... It's Ms. Jones on hot 97 in the morning y'all.

MEET THE DEFENDANTS

O kay. It would be real easy for me to sit in this cell and tell y'all that my fucked up childhood is what got me where I am today. Yeah, I could blame it on my mother and say that she was a crack head, a junkie and a prostitute. I could tell y'all how at the tender age of nine or ten she let dirty old men crush every ounce of innocence I had left in me, just so she could get a high. How she would go on weeklong disappearing acts and leave me in a filthy apartment. That was what I knew as home, all by myself, with no food or clean clothes.

Oh…don't forget the father story. How many times have you heard it? My daddy was an alcoholic who worked a dead end job. He came home from work, beat mommy and yelled and screamed because the house wasn't clean enough or dinner wasn't ready.

You know the drill on the late night. I'm his beautiful little angel. I'm daddy's princess. The only thing he did right in his life. So, it's okay for him to come lay in my bed in a drunken slumber, reeking of Old Spice and Wild Irish Rose. How he forced his smelly manhood in my mouth tore open my little vagina and greedily licked the stench of me off his ashy fingers when he took them out from inside of me.

Or, maybe y'all want to hear that because I went to school every day smelling like a toilet, the teachers reported my parents to the Department of Children and Family Services and the social workers came and took me out of that rat and roach infested place where the hallways were pain'ted with the smell of urine.

I could tell you about how weed smoke would fill the air so heavily that it made it hard to see the steps in front of you. I could go on and on with the fucked up childhood story but to keep it real with y'all, that's not what happened at all. Don't get me wrong, I grew up in the projects; but it wasn't that bad.

My mom was a beautiful Hispanic and black woman. She worked long hours as a nurse and made sure I had everything I could possibly want. It wasn't hard for her and my dad to provide for me being that I was an only child. My room was packed with the latest clothes and footwear, I always stayed three steps above the rest.

My father was a good dude. He was Cuban and black. He always talked real loud. I never knew why, he just did. I really was his little princess. No, he didn't touch on me or no shit like that. He was well respected by the guys in the neighborhood and you could always find him tryna talk some sense into the young boys around our way. He and my mom were together since eleventh grade. He was her first, her last and her only. My mom found out she was pregnant with me during their senior year. My dad found a night job working for his uncle and he continued to go to school to finish out his final year. He never left our side like most guys his age do.

When I was about seven or eight, I remember my aunt picking me up from school. Her eyes were red and swollen like she had been crying all day. No matter how many times I asked why she was crying, she wouldn't tell me. I later found out that my mom and dad were killed.

Supposedly my dad wasn't a nine-to-five dude. He was on the receiving end of large shipments of cocaine that was coming from Cuba to the U.S. Two days before he was killed he went to make a pick up but the crates were empty when he got there to unload them. My dad was nervous and didn't call the guy he was supposed to drop off the shipment to until the next day. The guy had my dad killed thinking he was tryna play him out of twenty thousand kilos. It just so happened that my dad was picking up my mom early from work that fateful day. When they got to him, they shot up the car, killing both my mother and father at the same time.

6

Our apartment in the projects was a front for the Feds to throw them off. So was my moms' job. Being so young, I didn't know the deal back then. I guess that explained our lavish living in the PJ's.

After my parent's death, I went to stay with my aunt and uncle and their three kids. My dad had a large sum of money stashed away that only his brother knew about. You would think being that they were supposed to be raising me with it, I should've been okay, right? Wrong. Those greedy bastards did nothing for me. They moved into a bigger home supposedly so I could have my own room. But, all I had was the basics. They were running through my dad's money and could care less about my ass. I vowed that once I got out of there, I would never look back.

How the fuck these muthafuckas gonna deny us any bail? Talking about we a flight risk. My attorney even tried to get them to put it at a mill flat and they still denied it. It really didn't matter to me how much it cost, fuck it. I got it, just give me a number. But I guess these pigs aren't as dumb as they seem. Because if they were, we damn sure woulda been bouncin' on them. Fuck a trial.

They got me in this cold ass box. I'M FUCKING FREEZING! I still don't know where we went wrong. I mean shit, we tried to be as smart as possible with our shit but it's the game. No matter how careful you think you are, the streets are always watchin'. These idiots even tried to get me to turn state; talkin' about if I testified for the prosecution, I would only do like eight years.

What they don't know is that without my girls, ain't no life for me out there no way. So what's the point? I ain't no fuckin' snitch. Plus, ain't no one person bigger than another in our clique. We all did the dirt together and reaped the benefits together. If we fall; then we'll fall together.

I never knew what family was until I met up with my girls in high school. When I came out the womb my mother left me at the hospital. I never knew her, my dad or any of my family for that matter. There is only two things in life I'm grateful to my moms for. One, she didn't abort me and two; she didn't leave me in a garbage or nuthin' like that.

I was in and out of different group and foster homes all my life. They were all supposed to just be temporary placements until they found me a permanent one. That day came when I was about fifteen. The social worker came to my school and told me she found me a new home and she had already gotten all of my belongings from the foster home. I was kind of mad because she didn't even give me a chance to say bye or nuthin'. I had an attitude all the way there. When we pulled up I already knew I was gonna have a problem at this new spot. A bunch of girls were sitting on the steps outside lookin at me all sideways.

One girl immediately started talking shit saying, "Man, we a got another new girl. I hope they don't put her in my room."

I held my tongue though because she didn't say that shit directly to me. After all the introductions and them taking me on a tour of the place, they showed me to my room.

Sure 'nuff it was the loud mouth bitch from outside in my room. She started asking me mad questions while I was unpacking my stuff. I kept ignoring her until she got so mad that she threw my CD player.

I grabbed that lil bitch by the neck and yoked her up against the wall. Then I threw her down on the floor and started stomping her. All the while yelling, "Bitch, you don't know me like that to be fuckin' with me or throwin' my stuff around! I will beat ya ass up in here!"

One of the workers came flying in the room and pulled me off her.

"Solace, what's the matter with you? You just got here and already you're fighting. Your case worker told me you had a temper, but this is unacceptable."

"It ain't my fault. She got mad cuz I don't feel like talkin' to her and she broke my CD player. I ain't do nuthin' to her for her to mess with my shit!"

"You watch your mouth young lady. We don't tolerate that type of language here. Is this true, Iesha? Did you break her CD player?"

"No, I ain't touch her stuff. She just started hittin' me."

"Bitch, you lying!" I shouted.

"Solace, I will not tell you again about using profanity."

"Whatever...she lying, and somebody gonna get me another CD player or we gonna have issues in this place," I replied.

"The both of you are on restriction for the week. You are to come straight home from school and go directly to your room. You will only be allowed out of your rooms during dinner and for your showers. Maybe the two of you will learn to get along then."

9

"What the hell is this jail? I ain't on any restriction! She's the one who broke my stuff; she got what she was lookin' for." I told the worker desperately.

"Finish unpacking your things and clean up this mess y'all made," the worker replied as she walked out of the room.

I continued to put my stuff away mumbling about how they got me fucked up around here.

"And, bitch, you paying for my CD player. My case worker told me we get ten dollars a week here for allowance; better believe I'm takin' yours all month."

"Whatever," said my new roommate, Iesha.

The first day at my new high school was cool. That's when I met Jada. We sat next to each other in homeroom and she asked me where I was from and all that. She gave me the four-one-one on everybody who was somebody and who was nobody.

She complimented me on my COOGI dress and Steve Madden boots my girl from the last youth home I was in boosted for me. We talked about the latest fashions. I loved the BCBG jogging suit she was wearing; it was black velour and had crystals spelling out BCBG across the front and down the leg. She had on a grey wife beater underneath the jacket and some grey, white and black Air Force Ones. She somehow made the whole fit look classy, even though it was a warm up suit.

By lunch, I had told Jada my life story and she told me hers. I've never felt so close to anyone in my life. She was so cool and listened to every detail. When I told her I had no family; she told me from that point on I had a sister for life. Jada told me how the only family she had were her aunt, uncle and cousins and also how much she hated them.

We made a pact together; as soon as we were old enough, she would rid herself of them, and I would rid myself of the system. We hung out every day from that point on. I was on restriction for the first week so I would sneak her in the house and we would hang out in the room. I dared Iesha to say something. She was cool with it though because she was just as bored as I was. I guess she figured if you can't beat 'em, join 'em. We all knew she couldn't beat me so she kept her mouth shut and Jada and I became inseparable.

ANGEL

I still haven't let the thought of *life* sink into my head. After being in here for six months, I've realized this isn't just a bad dream that I can wake up from. I'm really locked down and these people ain't playing. They want us locked up for the rest of our lives.

It's the murders that are holding us here. The other charges we could've gotten a bail on. But how the fuck do they know about any of them? We handled all of them like professionals and there's no way they have the bodies. Our clean up was too tight for that. No one knew it was us who did them. The streets didn't even know. Everyone was just reported as missing by friends and family. They never found anyone dead. So, how the fuck do they know?

Our lawyer keeps telling us the same thing...that we are going to beat this case, but I just don't know. The evidence against us is all circumstantial and hearsay. The jury will not sentence us to life with what little evidence they do have. But all the hype is suppose to be over some surprise witness they claim to have. Whoever it is, they can't know too much so we're not really worried about it. But the prosecution seems to be basing their whole case around it.

If they found a snitch somewhere, they better not blink for one second and let that muthafucka out of their site. Because guaranteed; if we find out who it is, their whole family is going to come up missing.

I hope my girls are holding up okay. I know Lace probably cool. She's a psycho for real. She probably sitting there like "my lawyer a beast... we gon' beat this trial then back to the paper chase."

Jada is strong but she's like me; and if we on the same page, then it's starting to be too damn real in here.

I love these chicks though. We been riding together for like almost ten years so it ain't gon' stop now. I know my girls strong in their spot and they're not going to give up no info, no plea-bargains, nothing. We've always been that way.

I remember when I first met Jada and Lace. They were so-phomores and I was a freshman. I was in the hall getting a book out of my locker when I heard Jada tell some girl that she didn't have to worry about her wanting some boy named Kareem.

"Y'all, bitches, burnt out. He the one tryna holla at me swee-tie; but make no mistake about it, I don't waste my time on these clowns in here. I am not about to stand here and argue with you over no nigga. That ain't *even* me."

The girl continued to run her mouth while Jada walked off. Later on, when we got out of school, there was a huge crowd out-side in front of the building. I saw the girl in the middle of a bunch of chicks talking about, "wait till that bitch come out."

When Jada came out the building and saw them she walked down the steps like it was nothing to her that five girls were wait-ing to fight her.

"I know y'all don't think y'all gon' jump me and get it off?" Jada asked pointedly.

"Bitch, ain't nobody gotta jump you! I got this by myself!" Replied the girl from the confrontation earlier that day.

"I'm not about to stand here and fight you over no nigga. Es-pecially, one that I don't even want."

"Bitch, you think you all that and I'ma be the one to...." Sud-denly, it was going down. She never got a chance to finish what she was saying. Jada punched her dead in her face while she was in mid-sentence.

Jada threw her on the ground and started kicking her all in her head saying, "Bitch, I told you, I don't argue with bitches and you still want to disrespect me!"

Just then, the girl's friends jumped in. I don't know why but I jumped in the fight to help out Jada. She had two of the girls by herself. Next thing I knew, Lace came out of nowhere and started swinging on everybody including me. When it was all said and done, we fucked them up. It was five against three and they still got their ass whooped.

After the fight, Jada and Lace asked me who was I and why did I jump in.

"I hate chicks like that. Always want to fight over some nigga and like to talk real loud for the crowd."

"I'm just like you girl, I don't like to argue. If you wanna bang, let's bang." Lace said.

"Yeah, but you don't know me so why you jump in and put ya'self out there like dat?" Jada asked seriously.

"I guess because I knew what they was gonna do, I think dat's some punk shit. It doesn't take five females to fight one girl, so I jumped in."

"That's what it is," said Lace, fixing her hair back. She had a long ponytail that was coming out from being pulled.

"What's ya name?" asked Jada.

"Angel."

"My name is Jada; this is Solace, we call her Lace."

We went back and forth finding out about each other until the sun went down. Next thing I knew, it was five-thirty pm and I knew I was gonna be in for it when I got home.

We agreed to meet up the next day and parted ways.

When I got home I could hear my mother yelling from the hallway. I could tell she was drunk again from the slurred way her words came out.

"And where is that little whore at? She ain't get here yet. I'ma put this size nine in her ass soon as she walks through the door."

I sat in the hallway for about another hour before going in. I figured she would be passed out by then and I could avoid the ass whooping until tomorrow. When I didn't hear anything anymore except the T.V. blasting I knew she was asleep.

I went in, made me a peanut butter and jelly sandwich and went to my room. I didn't have a real bed, just a mattress on the floor with a fitted sheet and a comforter on it. My window was covered with the flat sheet. My dresser was compliments of Ms. May who lived down the hall from us. It was all chipped up and the drawers were broke, but it held my clothes. I had a seventeen-inch television at the foot of my bed and a tiny radio next to it.

I turned on the radio and listened to Hot 97. I sat and thought about how bad I wanted a new life. I heard Jada and Laces stories, so I guess it could be worse. I could've been left at the hospital and not known my mother at all. But maybe that wouldn't have been so bad. Anything had to be better than getting hit for nothing. Or better than not eating at all some days because your mother spent up the money she had on liquor and sold the food stamps for money to buy even more liquor.

I knew once I was old enough, I was gonna be out for good. And from what I heard, Jada and Lace felt the same way.

We were together every day after that. Some days I got my ass whooped and others I'd wait until my mother fell asleep in hopes that she would have forgotten by the next day. It didn't matter because for once in my life, I wasn't alone. These girls became my family. They even started giving me some money to eat. They hated the bruises on my body from the constant beatings.

Eventually, I had to stop hanging out after school and hook up with them on the weekends. But from that first day and that first fight, we been fighting together ever since. Now, we're on trial together fighting for our lives.

JADA

For as long as I could remember, I had the mind of a hustler. Maybe it came from my dad. I was always thinking of ways to make money and get out of my aunt and uncles house. I could've done what every other chick around my way did. Fuck with a hustler and stay ghetto fabulous, but nah, that wasn't me. I needed more than hair, nails, and shoe money. Fuckin' with them nigga's like that, all I would end up is somebody's baby mother.

Besides, I wasn't feelin' any little nickel and dime nigga anyway. If I was gonna fuck wit' a hustler, I didn't even want the guy the nickel and dimers got their weight from. I wanted the nigga that the weight man's- weight man got his shit from at least. The rest was for the birds.

By my senior year, word on the street was that I thought I was better than everyone else. *Jada's stuck up, Jada's conceited*, you know how that goes. It didn't matter though. I was use to muthafuckas hatin' on me by then. I wasn't just pretty lil Jada no more. I had developed a body that people would pay sick money to have.

I stand five- eight and one hundred and forty five pounds. I have beautiful full lips, deep brown eyes, and ass for years and long hair. My legs command attention when I halt. My complexion shows that I'm of a mixed breed so it's a *fact* that I'm a bad bitch, it ain't even about being conceited. The bottom line is, I wanted more and I was determined to get it.

After I graduated high school, I wasn't too beat for the college thing. I had two best friends, I knew how to read, write, add, subtract, multiply and divide. What the fuck else did I need to know? I had money on my mind and college wasn't gonna get me that.

My girls and I planned on getting us a lil job and finding a crib of our own. We were trying to be out by the age of eighteen.

We all found a job working for this telemarketing company. They paid us ten dollars an hour, plus commission. All we had to do is call people and convince them to switch phone companies. Like I said, we had a hustler's mentality so we could convince a cow to buy milk if needed. The job served its purpose. We saved up some money and found an apartment soon after. I guess you could say that this is where all the madness began.

I saw an ad in the newspaper for brand new, three bedroom and two bath townhomes being built. I called the realty company for more information and to set up a viewing. The girl on the phone told me all we needed to bring was a photo id, two recent pay stubs and a thousand dollars for a security deposit. She told us if we liked the place that's all we would need to rent it. Simple enough I thought. We all went to see it and agreed it would be perfect for us.

The girl handling the paperwork was a fairly young girl like us. Her name was Symone. She was about five-eleven, slim build, about a size six, brown skinned with a spikey short haircut. She made copies of all of our information and told us the house would be ready in two months. After we left, my hustler's instinct kicked in.

"Yo, y'all saw how easy it was to rent that spot?" I asked.

"Yeah, it was," replied Lace. "I can't wait to move in."

"Me too, but that's not what I mean. I think we could make some money doing the same thing."

"You wanna get a job working for them?" Angel laughed.

"Nah, I wanna scam muthafuckas out a G." I replied.

"Oh shit! I get it now. You wild, Jada," said Lace.

"Damn, there goes our bus," said Angel. "Run, so we can catch it."

Once me and the girls boarded the bus, I continued explaining my newly thought up hustle.

"Look, what if we ran an ad in the newspaper saying the same thing. New houses being built and all that. We can get that girl Symone to send us some pictures of the one we saw and act like that's what the houses are gonna look like. To make it look legit, we tell people they have to bring identification and pay stubs like we did. We tell 'em its gon' take two months but it's on a first come first serve basis. If they want it, they have to leave the security deposit."

"Ok, sounds good, but where the people gonna come to? We don't have an office." Angel said.

"I know, that's the part I haven't figured out yet," I replied. "But when I do, it's on and poppin'."

"Why we don't just rent a lil office space?" said Lace.

"Yeah, but we can't rent it in our names. We need somebody else to sign the papers for it and we just do what that girl Symone is doing. Being that we only got two months from the time they come in, we have to get as many people as we can to fill out the application and leave the deposit," said Angel.

"I wonder if that girl Symone would be down to make some money. She probably knows a lot about this and could help. I'ma holla at her and see where her head is at. If she don't seem like the type I ain't even gonna bother. We just gon' make it happen," I told them.

We rode the rest of the way on the bus in silence. Everyone in deep thought about our lil scam idea.

Angel was thinking about how fucked up it would be to take money from the people who had kids. Here they are trying to keep a roof over their heads and we would be taking their money. Just as quick as the thought entered her mind she let it go. Angel knew we wouldn't give two shits about it. It's always about the dough so she let it ride.

When I got home I called Symone. To my surprise, Symone was as scandalous as we were and she was down with our plan. She agreed to meet up with me the next day and even said she had someone who could rent the space for us. Symone told me she was just a temp at the realty place; this was her last week so she needed the money.

I hated bringing people in on what my girls and I did, but Symone seemed genuine and I didn't get any bad vibes from her. We met up the next day after everyone got off work and went to the local pizza spot where we hung out to talk.

"I been thinking about doing somethin' like this for a while now. I ain't have nobody to help roll it out, so I guess we all met at the perfect time," Symone began.

"Jada, after you and I hung up last night, I called my brother to see if he would rent the space. He's a nut but he's cool. He just came home three months ago and already making fake ID's for people and stuff, so he gon' get somebody to rent it."

"What he was locked up for?" asked Lace.

"Girl, some bull-shit. He and his boys robbed Popeye's Chicken on Main Street. The crazy thing is they didn't even want the money, they just took it anyway. They held a gun to the people and had them make four hundred pieces of chicken and biscuits for a party they was having. I told you girl, he a nut."

We all burst out laughing so hard everybody in the pizza place turned to look at us.

"Okay, I found an office on Kennedy for rent. It's six hundred a month and being that we only need it for like two months, the guy giving us a month to month lease agreement," said Angel.

"Aiight. Y'all want my brother to make that happen tomorrow then?"

"Yeah, here go the information right here," Angel said, as she dug in her coat pocket for the piece of paper she wrote it on.

"What name y'all want it to be?" asked Symone

"How about if we call it *Easy Rentals Management?*" Lace asked, because this will be easy money?" She laughed.

"The crazy thing is, I like it," I told her.

We all laughed at the name this time.

"Ok, that's out the way, so how y'all wanna work the schedule? Somebody gotta be there," said Lace.

"I can do it. I know y'all have to work. Then y'all can alternate and come after work," Symone told us. "I think that might be good anyway, most places only stay open until like five o'clock so this will allow people to come later, when they get off work or whatever, you feel me?"

"Yeah, dat's Wass' up," I said.

"Nah, I think one of us should be there too. We need to know how many people came in so we know how much dough comes in everyday. Nuthin' against you Symone, but I think that's the best way to do it." Lace said.

"I'm cool wit' dat, ma. I just thought it would be easier for y'all, dat's all."

"Lace is right," said Angel. "I'll do it. I'm tired of that damn phone company anyway. I will be more than happy to quit."

"Shit, we gonna be making money anyway. I think it would be okay if you did," I said. "Lace and I will come after work."

"Okay, that'll work," said Symone.

"I'll set up the phones while I'm at work tomorrow. That way, we don't have a bill. I can credit it out," I laughed.

"You a scammin' ass bitch, you know that?" Angel laughed.

"Yup. Sure do bitch. But my scammin' ass ideas gonna keep us paid." I told her.

"Both of y'all stupid; and we all some scammin' ass bitches," said Angel. "Look right, we need some office furniture. Good thing tomorrow is Friday; we have a lot to do." Angel continued.

"We don't need nuthin' too extravagant, just some stuff to make it look good. We can rent everything from Rent – A - Center since we only need it for a lil while. The computers, the fax and copier, all that," I said.

"The same guy that rents the office can do that too. Shit he using fake information anyway, might as well do that also," said Symone. "I'll take care of that too."

"The only thing left is running the ad in the newspapers. I'll do that after the office is set and ready to go. We should have everything together by Monday." I thought out loud.

After we left the pizza spot, everything was in place for the realty scam. By this time next week we hoped to be making some dough.

The weekend flew by being that everybody was so busy getting things together. Before we knew it, it was Tuesday and the phones were already ringing off the hook. I had three lines added to make sure people could get through. By two o'clock, five people had already come in.

Symone and Angel had print outs of the townhouses laid out for people to view. Symone brought in the real blueprints from her old job that showed the different layouts to make it look good.

They told people they could drive by the location where the houses were being built if they wanted to see the neighborhood.

Everything was going smooth. They made photo copies of the applicants' information and they never suspected it was a scam. By the time me and Lace got there at five- thirty, they already had eight thousand dollars.

"Damn, eight people came in this bitch already?" Lace asked looking in the envelope where the money was.

"Yup," said Angel. "I hope it's like this every day. We gonna be sooooo paid."

"Oooh, girl, let me tell you about the chick that came in here with her "Section 8" voucher," said Symone. She had two bad ass kids wit' her. When I told her we didn't accept Section 8, she went off on me, talking about that's discrimination."

"That's crazy. I put in the ads *No Section 8*." I said.

"People are just slow," I laughed. "I also put that the deposit has to be in cash or money order, no personal checks. No exceptions y'all."

"Yeah, nobody tried to give us a check," said Symone.

Just then two people walked in wanting to fill out the application for a rental. They were sisters and asked if they could get two units next to each other. Lace and I watched as Symone and Angel went through the process with them. If we didn't know the shit was a scam then we would've been got too.

The office was set up perfect and the applications she picked up from *Staples,* made it look real good. While the people filled out the application, Symone and Jada made copies of their pay stubs and all that. When they were done and the people paid, they gave them a receipt and advised them that someone would contact them when the units were ready; however, it would be about another two months before they were finished.

Confident that we had the process down, me and Lace told Symone and Angel they could leave. We stayed at the office until eight pm, the closing time we advertised. When it was all said and done, we had made fourteen thousand dollars in one day.

Everyday got better and better and word was traveling fast about the new town- homes for a reasonable price. Every night before she left, Angel would log how much she and Symone made for the day and I did the same before leaving with Lace.

Symone handled the money orders every day. We paid the guy two thousand dollars a day to cash them and he was more than fine wit' that. We were bringing in about fifteen to twenty-thousand dollars a day with our scam. We didn't think it would be a good idea to rent the townhouse as we planned, so eventually, we went back and withdrew the application. We didn't want people coming around and asking questions when it was all said and done.

After the two months was up, we closed the office as scheduled. As much as we didn't want to, we had to. We knew being greedy is how people get caught most of the time. We didn't stop though. We just opened an office in a different city and kept it going. After two months we closed it. We did that for another six months. By then it was on the news and in the papers about the scam so people knew the deal. They still didn't know who was responsible for it though. All they had was descriptions and not very good ones at that.

By the time it was all said and done, we had made over half-million dollars off the realty scam. All money was equally divided between the four of us after expenses and we were good. Symone became a part of our crew from that moment on. We still kept our jobs though. Not because we needed the money, we didn't want to draw any type of attention to ourselves so we continued to work. It later proved to be a smart move on our end. Having that job is what set up our next big scam.

JADA

We got settled in our new house about a month after the realty scam. We found a beautiful four-bedroom house in Scranton that had a full finished basement. It had central heat and air, a laundry room and a great room separate from the family room. It had an eat- in kitchen and the dining room was also separate. The upstairs had three bedrooms and two bathrooms.

Symone decided to move in with us, so she took the basement. It had another bedroom, a bathroom, living room and laundry room down there. We paid the sixteen hundred dollar a month rent; for the full year in advance, so the owner had no problem renting to us. He didn't ask any questions after he heard we wanted to pay in advance.

About six months later is when our next scam came into play. Angel started fucking with this guy name Crook. The name suited his ass perfectly. He and his boys made fake credit cards. They took people's real information and made duplicate cards. It worked out because the people weren't missing the card itself. They didn't know what was going on, by the time they realized something was wrong and cancelled the card, thousands were already spent.

Once I found out about what he did, I knew we had to get in on it somehow. We deal with credit card information all day every day at work, so it would be nothing to get it. We just had to be smart about our shit. So after I figured the best way to do it, I told the girls.

I found Lace in her room watching the movie *"Set It Off"*. Soon as I walked in, I already knew what she was gonna say. The same shit she says every time she watches that movie.

"Wass' up, Lace?" I asked, ready for her speech.

"I'll tell you wass' up. We need to rob a mutha-fuckin' bank, dats wass' up." Lace replied, not taking her eyes off of the movie.

"Bitch please! Every time you watch that shit you wanna rob a fuckin' bank. We ain't robbing no bank," I said as I hit her with the pillow off her bed. Gimmie that fuckin' movie cuz, every time you watch it you get all amped and wanna be them."

"I don't wanna be them. Those bitches got killed." Lace laughed. "Whatever, dis my movie anyway."

"I know, but we ain't robbin' no bank for the ten millionth time. But I'm glad you in grind mode, I got an idea," I continued. "You know how dat nigga Crook and 'em get down right? We need to get in on that, fa real."

"What y'all doin'? " Angel jumped in as her and Symone walked in the room.

"Jada scheming ass plottin' again," laughed Lace.

"Word! On what?" Symone asked.

I told them about my idea and how we should do the same thing.

"I'm wit' that Jada, but I don't wanna run wit' any niggas like that. If we do this, then we do our own shit our way," said Lace.

"Girl, you already know," I said.

"Okay, but they the ones with the machines to make the shit. Fuck y'all want me to do, steal the shit?" Angel asked.

"Nah, you ain't gotta steal it. The machines are in his house, right?" I asked.

"True. I saw one for Visa and one for MasterCard." Angel said.

"Oh! I see where you going Jada," said Symone

"Exactly!" I said smiling. "Watch that nigga while he makin' that shit every chance you get. Let us know when you ready.

"In the meantime, this is what I want y'all to do. Every day at work, I want y'all to take down two people's card information, make sure they have a high credit rating. If they don't have A-1 credit, don't bother. Do everything the same as far as confirming the information, but don't put the order through. After you got all they info, tell 'em it's not going through; but you think it's ya system, so you're gonna transfer the call so they can be set up. That way it can't come back that you took that call."

"Aiight dats wass' up," Lace said.

"Angel, you gotta be slick wit' ya shit. However you choose to get to those machines is on you, just be careful and don't let Crook catch you," said Symone.

"Yeah, I would hate to have to put sumthin hot in him," said Lace.

We all laughed as Lace made a gun motion with her fingers.

"Yeah okay, Cleo." I laughed.

"Oh, she been watchin' set it off again, huh?" said Angel. "Every fuckin' time. It never fails. Then you start runnin' around here like you a killa or somethin'. Fuck outta here."

We all laughed hysterically.

For the next two weeks Angel spent as much time as she could watchin' Crook. She was careful not to make it obvious. When she was sure she knew how to do it, she waited until Crook made a run and made a dummy card just to make sure she had it down. The card looked real as hell, she couldn't wait until she got home so she could show us.

"Damn, this look official as hell," I said. "How long did it take to make it?"

"Girl, that's the thing. It is takin' Crook like half an hour to make 'em. I made this shit in ten minutes."

"Okay cool, we have a bunch of cards for you," I said.

"Listen, this how I'ma do it. Crook has to go out of town Saturday. He usually locks his equipment in his safe. I'ma do as many as I can tonight. I'ma act like I'm sick and send him to the store. Then when he comes back, I'ma act like he got the wrong thing and send his ass back."

We all laughed.

"Then when he gets home I'ma tell him I just need to be in my own bed and have him bring me home."

"Damn girl, you ain't got no key to his apartment?" asked Symone.

"Bitch is you slow or something?" Angel teased. "Yeah I got a fuckin' key. I got that shit week two of me fuckin' wit' him. He was all like, 'I ain't givin' no female a key to my shit', and all that.

"After I fucked him, that nigga was singin' a whole different song. But I just told you, he locks it in the safe. Before you ask bitch, no, I ain't got no key to the safe. But you know a bitch workin' on it. Don't worry, I got this. I'ma make some tomorrow and when he gets back I'll make the rest."

"Yeah, okay. And for the record bitch, I'm far from slow," said Symone.

"I don't know girl, we worry about you sometimes," I laughed.

That night, Angel's plan went better than she thought. If she was really sick she would've screamed on Crook for how long it took him to come back from the store. But she was happy he took over an hour. She didn't even have to send him back out. She made ten cards while he was gone. Soon as he got back, she asked him to take her home, just like she planned.

When she walked in the door she started singing out loudly, "*Weeeee goooin shoppin', weeeee goooin shoppin'.*"

We looked over the cards to make sure they all came out good. Everything was dead on so we were sure the cards would work.

"So wass' up...we going shoppin' tomorrow or what?" asked Lace while taking the pins out her hair from her doobie.

"Look y'all, we can't be stupid wit' this shit," I said. "We don't wanna be goin' from store to store shopping. They got cameras and shit and when shit hit the fan that's the first thing they check out. Where the cards were used and then get the tapes from the stores. So we can't do it like that."

"Bitch, you watch *waay* too much of those CSI type of shows on TV," said Angel.

"Damn right I watch that shit. If you ask me, those shows teach a criminal minded bitch like me how to do shit and get away wit' it. They show you every little fuckin' thing they look for so you know how to be more careful."

"It's the truth though," Symone jumped in.

"So how you think we should do it then? You wanna wear disguises?" Angel laughed.

"Yeah, why not. We can't trust anybody to come in wit' us. Muthafuckas get shook and start runnin' they mouth when shit hit the fan, so fuck all lat. I'm not takin' any chances of bringin' anybody else in. So we gonna shop ourselves and yeah, we gonna wear disguises."

"Cool wit' me. I'm getting all types of shit too. Where y'all wanna shop at?" said Symone. "And when?"

"Tomorrow let's try easy shit to get a feel of it and make sure the card's good. Let's go buy clothes and shoes and stuff like that before we go fuck wit' big shit," said Lace.

"See now you're thinking, tomorrow it's on and poppin," I said while giving my girls high fives.

Our credit card thing was working perfectly. We all went to different stores that following day and none of us had any problems at the register. We even had Symone's brother make us some fake ID's to go along with all the cards. That helped out a lot when it came to making large purchases. That's about the only time those stupid ass people in the stores asked for ID. After a while, we had more clothes and shoes along with anything else than you could possibly imagine. The money from our jobs was nothing but we kept it anyway to continue to get card info. Our house looked like a fuckin' *Cribs* episode. But even though we had all that material stuff, we still didn't have a cash flow.

We started buying stuff to sell to make money but the money was nowhere near where we needed it to be. We were only making about five thousand dollars a week selling everything from clothes to electronics. We even bought furniture sets for people and charged them half the price. We had customers all over P.A. that we delivered to. We would meet people at different locations because we didn't want anyone knowing where we lived.

Roughly seven months later, Angel got a call. Crook was locked up and we were devastated. The Feds took everything, including his equipment. When they started airing that shit on the news about all the complain't s people were making to the credit card companies, they put all that shit on Crook and his crew. The Feds thought everything came back to his team somehow. They had no idea it was two separate groups working the same scam and that's exactly how we needed it. But his bust stopped our flow. We no longer had the equipment to make the cards.

A short while later is when we met Zy, I knew from day one she was gonna be our ticket to get sick money.

JADA

Lace and I were in the grocery store doing some shopping with a dummy card, of course. With the cart packed we found what looked like the shortest line of people waiting. The white lady at the head of the line was just about finished and there was only one other person ahead of us. When it was her turn, she placed the jars of baby food on the counter along with the cans of milk, Huggies diapers and baby wipes.

"Forty-two dollars and sixty-four cents," said the cashier.

The girl handed her two twenty-dollar bills and three singles. The cashier looked at the bills then marked them with a marker.

"These bills aren't real," said the cashier as she handed them back to the girl.

"What?! How you gon' tell me my money fake?" she snapped.

"I didn't say they were fake but these bills aren't real either, mam," the cashier insisted.

"You must've lost ya mind, lady. I don't have time for this, so are you gonna ring me up or what?" the girl asked in an irate tone.

"I cannot accept these bills," she said with an aggravated expression looking at the now long line of people waiting. "I'm sorry but there's nothing more I can do."

"Ain't shit wrong with my money. Why you ain't give that white lady who just left a problem? You ain't look at her money all funny and mark up the bills like you did me. That's some racist ass shit," she said snatching the money from the counter.

An elderly man came over to the register to see what all the commotion was about. His hair was graying and he wore thick glasses. I assumed he was the manager.

"Is there a problem, Laurie?" he asked the cashier.

"The bills she gave me aren't real and she thinks I'm being racist." The cashier responded.

"The fat bitch *is* being racist 'cause ain't a damn thing fake about my money. But it's all good, I'll go spend my money elsewhere," the girl stormed off.

"Miss, if you could just hold on a minute I'm sure we can resolve this," said the elderly man.

"It ain't shit to resolve. I ain't shopping here no more and I'ma call the newspapers and tell them how racist this grocery store is," the angry customer said as she stormed off.

I watched the girl walk out the store while the cashier put the items she was trying to purchase off to the side.

"Miss, you can add that stuff to my purchase," I told her.

"What you doin'?" Lace asked. "What you gon' do wit' some pampers and wipes?"

"I got an idea," I whispered to her.

We paid for the stuff and walked outside just as the girl was getting in her car.

"Hey! Excuse me!" I yelled.

She rolled her window down and looked at me with an attitude.

"Do I know you?" she asked.

"Nah. But I saw the lady givin' you a hard time. I got ya stuff for you. I figured you must need it," I told her sincerely.

"You ain't have to do that, ma."

"It's cool, it was nuthin'. My name is Jada by the way, this is my girl Lace." I said motioning to Lace.

"I'm Zy, short for Zyasia."

"Can I ask you a question?" I asked while handing her the bag with the pampers and wipes and stuff.

"Yeah, wass' up?" she asked as she reached out and accepted the bags.

"Are the twenties real or fake?" I asked seriously.

Zy giggled. "What y'all the police or some shit?"

"Girl, we far from that," Lace replied.

"Yeah, it's counterfeit. I been tryna make this shit for a while now but it still ain't right. I need some stuff to get it there but that shit cost too much. I been tryna to make it work wit' out it to make 'em look real. But as y'all can see, it still ain't working," she laughed.

"Well look, we might be able to help you wit' that but I don't wanna stand out here and talk about it," I told her.

"Girl the stuff I need cost like four thousand dollars all together. How y'all gonna help wit' dat?"

"That ain't the point, ma. The question is, if you had all the stuff you needed, could you get it right?" Lace asked.

"Yeah, it would be dead right then," said Zy.

"Aiight; cool, then take my cell number and give us yours. We can get together and make it happen," said Lace.

"Dats wass' up." Zy told us.

They exchanged numbers and Zy started her car to leave.

"Thanks again for the pampers and stuff." Zy told us gratefully.

"Call us and next time we see you, you not gon' have to worry about pampers for as long as ya baby wear them, girl," I said.

"Aiight, fa sho' then. I'ma get at y'all. Lata."

When we got back to the house, we told Angel and Symone about Zy.

"Get the fuck outta here girl," said Angel.

"Hell yeah," said Lace. "So if we get this right, this gonna put us on a whole 'nother level, fa real."

"And y'all good wit' this chick gettin' down wit' us?" asked Symone.

"I mean, it's a lot that has to be worked out. We don't know the chick at all, so we gotta see how her mind work you know. See if she just some lil grinder or if she tryna get money," I said. "If her head on right and she turn out to be strong in her spot, we might just have to put her down wit' us you know. I mean, we gotta wait and see what happens. Shit, we might not ever talk to shorty again. Who knows?"

"If it works out it could be good for all of us!" said Symone.

"Yes but we can't call it. For all we know she on some bullshit, let's just wait and see," I told my girls and we all agreed to wait and see how this would play out. I don't like building up false hopes, especially when it comes to my clique.

Two days later, Zy called and we made arrangements to meet after work. We still weren't trying to let nobody know where we lived, so we met up at her house. She had a small one-bedroom apartment in a run-down, dilapidated building on the other side of town.

To our surprise, when we walked in, the place smelled like Febreze, and she kept it really clean. Still, my first thoughts were if all goes well, we need to help find her a better spot for her and her baby.

The bedroom was very big and spacious. She had a basinet and a chest for the baby, a queen-sized bed and dresser and a computer desk in the corner. You could tell that she hooked her lil spot up the best she could.

"Y'all can have a seat in the livin' room. Y'all want somethin' to drink?"

"Nah, we good," said Lace.

"So, where's the baby?" I asked Zy.

"He's at my mothers' house. I asked her to watch him for me so we could talk wit' out no distractions. He can be a handful sometimes."

"Oh, okay. Well, maybe we can meet lil man next time then. So what's the deal wit' the money?" I asked her, getting right to the point.

"Well like I told y'all, I have been tryna make the money for a hot minute now. My brother was makin' it but he never really got a chance to get it going. He was killed earlier this year. Ever since then, I been tryna do it myself and pick up where he left off. He told me about this program he needed, but I been tryna do it wit' out it. Sometimes it works sometimes it doesn't. But if I really want it to work most of the time, I need the program. I just don't have the money for dat, you know. So I been tryna get it as good as I can wit' out it."

"Let me see some," said Lace.

Zy showed them on her computer how she made the counterfeit money. Then, she pulled out a few bills so we could get a good look at it. Lace and I looked at the bills real close.

"I ain't no expert or nuthin ma, but I can see from the door two problems already. The paper is too thin and the color too dark," I told her.

"I know. The colors are much better on the program I was telling y'all about, the graphics and everything. I've tried like five different types of paper," she told us.

"Aiight, look right," said Lace. "We can get you everything you need to get it right but from this point on we all a team. We all partners on this and loyalty is key in anything we fuck wit', you know? So we need to know that we can trust you no matter what. Cuz where we wanna take this can start to raise a lot of eyebrows. Feel me? If anything ever happens, you gotta know to never talk and we got you. We a family and we ride for each other, so if you wanna be a part of this team like we want you to be, then that's the cards all laid out for ya. We can get money, fa real you know?"

"I feel you," said Zy. "I have a lil man to think about and this nine-to-five ain't gettin' it. I'm tryna make moves for me and my son. I told y'all I been at this for a minute now, so I'm wit' y'all if y'all wit' me."

"Aiight, well enough said." Lace told her.

"Hit us up tomorrow so we can go get the stuff and we want you to meet Angel and Symone also when you have time." I told her. "It's important that we all meet and be on the same page."

We were getting ready to leave when she said, "Ok cool then, I'll leave out wit' y'all. I gotta go pick up Jalen from my mother."

The next morning, Lace and I got up early to go to Wal-Mart. We bought mad cases of pampers and wipes for the baby. We needed three carts just for that alone. We wanted to make sure she didn't run out anytime soon. We also bought cases of milk and baby food. Then we went to the mall and got him so much stuff we had to make two trips to get it all to the taxi.

Once we had everything we needed, we headed to Zy house so we could go shopping for the stuff she needed to make the money. When we got there, she had just finished dressing herself and was getting the baby together. She saw all the stuff we had and couldn't believe it.

"Damn, y'all bought all this for me?" she looked at all the bags in disbelief. "Y'all didn't have to do that. This had to cost a grip. Look at all this stuff," she said in awe.

"Girl, it was nuthin'. We got it cheaper than you know, trust me," Lace replied.

"Thank y'all sooo much. I'ma put one of his new outfits on him right now," Zy said smiling. "So, can I ask y'all something?"

"Wass' up?" I replied.

"Y'all can't be doin' it like that workin' for the phone company. I mean the way y'all dress and everything. All this designer stuff y'all are wearing. All this stuff y'all got Jalen. And now, y'all about to buy all this expensive stuff to make the money with. What y'all into?" she asked me seriously.

"Let's just say we have A-1 credit and leave it at that," replied Lace.

"Look, if we gonna be working together on this money thing then y'all should know y'all can trust me. I mean, I ain't in no position to run my mouth about nuthin'. I'm just tryna get it like y'all gettin' it, feel me? I have a baby to take care of and my job ain't gettin' it. That's why I be tryna do this on the side you know…to make ends meet."

"Well trust me when I tell you girl," I said. "If all goes well, you gonna be doing a whole lot more than makin' ends meet. We haven't lied to yet have we? We told you the next time you saw us you wouldn't have to worry about ya lil man and pampers or none of dat. We told you we would be here to go get the stuff you need and we here, right? So just trust us on this. What we got going on right now ain't gonna be nuthin' compared to what we all about to do together. But if you want some new clothes so you can shine too then we can get that too, okay?"

"You a part of our team now and birds of a feather flock together. As you can see we flock very well so it's a must you do too. Plus, we shop a lot, so we need to always look like we can afford the shit we buying, you know? But girl, you ain't gonna have to worry about none of that in a minute. You and Jalen gonna be straight."

"Aiight, dats wass' up. I'm ready. Did y'all drive here?"

"Nah, we don't have a car," said Lace.

"Y'all ain't got no car?" asked Zy with surprise.

"By choice, but we about to get some cars," I said. "So if you don't mind, we ridin' wit' you."

"Nah, of course, y'all good. I'm just surprised dats all. But it's all good, let's go. I just need to drop Jalen off at my mother's first."

We dropped off the baby and went to Best Buy, then Staples. Zy got everything she needed down to the paper cutter. Zy wasn't lying when she said the stuff was really expensive. We bought two of almost everything to make certain we would be good. We spent seven thousand dollars on all that stuff. We charged it to two of the credit cards, so the money wasn't an issue.

The paper she needed was hard to find, so after about two hours we finally found it. The guy in Staples told us most stores don't carry it anymore. We finally found a stationary store up in "Whiteville" a real suburban part of P.A. that had it. I don't even know what city we were in, but it was definitely "Whiteville" if you ask me. We bought ten cases of it. Twenty packs per case. Zy was sure that was the right paper so we bought a lot.

By then it was about three o'clock, we went to the outlet stores so Zy could get some stuff. We took her to the mall after that and let her run wild. When we were done, it was seven o'clock. Even if it wasn't that late, nothing else would fit in her car anyway. We stopped to get somethin' to eat then went back to her house.

Zy threw all her new stuff on her bed and after all the thanks you's, she finally got to work on the computer. We watched her intensely as she installed programs, and set up the coloring and everything. The girl had skills and the more we watched her the more we knew we were about to get paid.

It took her about three hours to get it to what she thought was perfect. She had shots of real money on the screen that she had scanned and preloaded from before. Then we saw the image of a twenty-dollar bill appear next to the real bill on the screen and watched her hit print. She loaded the new paper in the printer and waited. When it came out she took the paper cutter out of the bag and cut the bill out.

"One of y'all got twenty dollars?" Zy asked.

Lace handed her a twenty and she held the bills together to compare them.

"*Daaaaamnn!*" Lace and I said in unison.

"It's hard to tell them apart, let me see them?" I asked her.

Zy handed me the bills and Lace and I examined them thoroughly. It wasn't exact, but it was the closest thing to it. The only difference was the color was a tiny bit darker than the real twenty. It wasn't obvious. You had to look real hard to catch it.

"Here…let me show y'all something," Zy said reaching for the bills.

She took a marker out her drawer and marked the bills. The color again was only a tad bit off.

"This is as close as it gets to real money, trust me. These lil imperfections ain't nuthin' compared to other counterfeit money I saw. Somebody gotta take a magnifying glass and inspect it to see a difference. Look at the other money compared to this."

She took out one of the first bills she created the day before and immediately they saw the difference.

"Yo, this is crazy. I don't see how you could get any closer though, Zy, so we good wit' dis right here," said Lace. "If I didn't just watch you make this, I wouldn't know it was counterfeit."

"I was just thinking the same thing," I told them.

"So, y'all want me to print it up then?" asked Zy.

"Hell yeah," they both said and laughed.

Zy printed one hundred pages of the money. She only used tens, twenties and fifties. She said the ones and fives were senseless to her and the hundred dollar bills were harder to get off so they would only work with those currencies. Of course, Lace and I were good with that.

While the bills printed, I thought it would be a good time to bring up somethin' that was on my mind.

"Zy, I wanted to holla at you. I just wanna make sure we all on the same page you know?"

"Fa sho, wass' up?"

"Look, being that you gonna have the stuff here to make the money, how we know you not gonna just dip off on us?" I asked.

"Yo real talk, Jada, I ain't even mad at you for askin'. But on some real shit, y'all been true to y'all word since day one. Y'all ain't have to do shit when y'all saw me in that store. But y'all looked out and kept it real wit' me. So why would I try to play y'all? I ain't gonna do y'all dirty like that at all. Like y'all said, we a team now. Plus, I'ma show y'all how to make it too so we all can be on the same level, you know. I may not be able to make it every chance we need, so I think we all need to be able to make it. You feel me?"

"Oh, no doubt you gonna show us how to make it?" asked Lace with a serious look on her face.

"Fa sho."

"Aight, well, I feel like you need us just as much as we need you so long as we got a understanding, we should be good." I said.

"I'm wit' y'all don't worry," said Zy.

For the next hour we cut out the money. The bills printed ten per page and we printed one hundred pages. We decided we wouldn't do anything until the following day, so we called a Taxi to get home. Zy offered to drop us off but we refused sayin' it was late and we would be fine. The real reason was we were skeptical about letting people know where we lived. Yeah Zy was a part of the team, but we wanted to make sure everything was cool with Angel and Symone before we broke that rule.

When we got home, it was close to one am and we didn't bother waking up Symone. Angel was in her bedroom wide-awake so we showed her the bills we brought with us and told her all about the day we had.

"You and that chick just made this wit' the stuff y'all got her?"

"Yup," replied Lace. "We gonna try it out tomorrow."

"Aiight," said Angel. "If this works, I got an idea too. But I'm tired so we can go over dat tomorrow."

"Yeah me too," I said. "I'll see y'all in the morning."

The next day, Symone came upstairs waking everybody up.

"Damn what time is it?" Lace asked, pulling the comforter over her head.

"It's twelve-thirty, get up. I even cooked for y'all bitches."

Then she came to me and Angel's rooms to wake us up.

After everybody washed their faces and brushed their teeth, they all met up downstairs in the dining room and ate breakfast together. Symone hooked it up. French toast, eggs, beef sausages and orange juice.

"Damn, let me call Zy and let her know we just got up," said Lace.

"Yeah," I replied handing her the cordless phone off the receiver in the kitchen.

"So, what happened yesterday?" asked Symone. "Y'all was gone all day and ain't call a bitch or nuttin'."

"She just woke up too," said Lace, "but she wanna know if we want her to meet us here," she whispered.

They all looked at each other.

"Hold on," Lace said into the receiver, "I'm tryna see what they wanna do."

"I was gonna ask y'all if y'all was cool wit'' her knowin' where we live?" Lace asked Angel and Symone.

"I mean, y'all met her, so what you think?" Angel asked. "You think she's all good?"

"Yeah, I think she's good people," I said.

Lace nodded her head in agreement.

"Aiight, so yeah, tell her to come through then." And tell her to bring dat wit' her," I said.

Lace gave her the address and she said she would be there soon. While they ate, Lace and I brought them up to speed on what happened the day before, and asked how they wanted to work our new get money project. We went over a few details and rounded things up.

"So, today we all gonna go out and see what the deal is wit' it?" Lace asked.

"Yeah, but if the money good we need to do more than run around in stores," said Angel. "I mean, of course we gonna shop and all, but we really could use this as a way to get some serious money. I think we should sell it."

"Sell it to whom?" Lace asked real properly, trying to be funny.

"I'm sure it's plenty of people who would buy it," said Symone. "I think that's a bangin' ideal."

"Yeah, but we don't have any clientele. What we gon' do, go around advertising we got counterfeit dough for sell? Y'all tryna get locked up?" I asked.

"Ain't nobody gonna get locked up. All we gotta do is plug the right people to what we got, the clientele gonna come to us, guaranteed," said Angel.

"Aiight, fuck it then, let's do this today and if we good, then let's make that happen," said Lace.

We finished breakfast and everybody showered and got dressed. I had on a white Vera Wang top with Alexander McQueen skinny jeans, a pair of white and gold Alexander McQueen sandals and white and gold Alexander McQueen purse. Lace had on a pair of Seven jeans with a black fitted Ed Hardy T-shirt and some black Ed Hardy tennis shoes and her oversized black Ed Hardy Bag. Angel came down wearing tight True Religion jeans with a black off the shoulder True Religion sweater. Her over sized Channel purse looked great with the Channel heels and sunglasses she wore. My girls and I stayed dressed. When Zy got there, Symone let her in and let her know we would be ready in a minute. Zy looked amazing in the Jimmy Choo outfit she picked out just the day before. She is one of us now, and we had to make sure she dressed the part. Zy walked around the house in awe of how beautiful it was.

To Zy, it looked liked some rich white people lived there. Not a bunch of twenty-year-old girls.

"Ya'll got mad flava to be so young," she said.

I wasn't sure but I had a feeling that she knew if things went well with the counterfeit money, she was definitely getting her and Jalen a new place.

When everyone was ready we piled in Zy's Nissan Altima and headed to the stores. We tried grocery stores, gas stations, clothing stores, and even the jewelry store.

We went through fast food drive thru's and asked people coming out of banks and check cashing places for change. The end result was the same everywhere. Nobody questioned the money. When they marked it, they still put in the registers and kept it moving.

"Yo, I wanna see somethin'," said Angel. "Zy, go to a check cashin' place right quick."

When she pulled up Angel got out.

"Gimmie five hundred dollars and mix it up." Angel said while leaning back into the car.

Five minutes later she came out the check-cashing place and got in the car. She handed Zy a money order for five hundred dollars and they all burst out laughing.

"You stupid," laughed Lace.

"No, they stupid," Angel laughed. "But dats wass' up...now we know."

"Wait, fuck that," said Zy. "I'll be right back."

She counted out fifteen hundred in twenty dollar bills and went in the check-cashing place. She too, came out with three money orders for five hundred dollars each.

"Shit, if it was that simple, then I might as well get my bill money," she said laughing.

"Girl, I ain't even mad at you," said Symone.

We laughed all the way back to the house. We talked about how dumb people were and how good the money was.

Once we were back at the house, we made some drinks with the stuff we got from the liquor store with our counterfeit money. Then we sat around to figure out our next move.

"I can't drink too much," said Zy, "I gotta go get Jalen from my mom in a few. I am so grateful that she takes him for me on weekends. She loves spending time with him and it gives me a chance to do what I need to, without lugging him around all the time."

Yeah, I feel you. Where is his father at?" Symone asked.

Girl, where else? Locked up. But he wasn't around when I was pregnant anyway. I can count on one hand how many times he saw Jalen when he was on the streets. When he did come around, it was only to try and fuck me. When he saw I wasn't beat, he stopped coming around."

"Damn. Some niggas ain't shit," I said.

"It's ok, Zy, cuz now Jalen got four new aunties," said Symone.

"Awe, dats Wass' up y'all," said Zy.

"So now that we know the dough good, how y'all want to do this?" Lace asked.

"Well, I was thinking about what Angel said earlier about selling it," said Symone.

"Yeah, I already got some people who want it," said Zy. "They were pressing me for minute but it wasn't right yet, so now that it is I can holla at them."

"Ok, I'll plug my brother so he can put the bug in the streets," said Symone.

"How much y'all want to charge for it?" Lace questioned.

"How about we double the amount of what they're spending?" I said. If they wanna spend five hundred, they get a G, if they want to spend a G, they get two G's and we make that the minimum, or people gonna have us running around like chickens wit' our heads cut off for fifty dollars."

"Hell yeah. You're right," said Lace. "That sound good to y'all?" She asked, looking around the living room.

"Yeah, that's cool," everyone agreed.

"Aiight, I'm a get on that then," Zy continued. "Right now I need to go pick up Jalen, so I'll call y'all this week. I know everybody gotta work, so we'll make arrangements to get together. Y'all hold on to the rest of what's printed up."

"Aiight girl, we'll see you later then. Call me," I said as I walked her to the door.

We all sat around drinking and joking around for a while before we went to our rooms to get ready for work the next day.

"Yo, how much longer we gonna work at this fuckin' place?" Lace asked, heading up the stairs.

"Girl, the way I'm thinkin', we about to get money, I'll give it a month tops," Symone laughed."

"That's about accurate," Angel said, shaking her head and laughing.

Wednesday came around and I hadn't heard from Zy yet. Symone's brother already had a few people lined up with orders. The hustlers were all over it and we just couldn't reach her. We had the money Zy left but we wanted to let her know first what we were gonna do. We didn't want to seem shady. Zy finally called them back on Thursday apologizing for not calling sooner. She explained that between work and the baby she's been real busy. She let me know she printed up some more money and she would drop it off on Friday.

"Was that her?" Lace asked.

"Yeah, she said she will be here Friday and she gonna install the program on our computer and show us how to do it," I relayed to the girls.

"Oh, you know the first thing I thought was shorty tryna dip on us," said Lace.

"Shit, me too girl," I replied.

Just then, Angel walked in the house with Symone in tow.

"Yo, look at this shit," said Symone. She was showing them two sheets of paper with names, numbers and amounts next to them.

"Damn, all those orders?" I asked.

"Hell yeah, where the fuck shorty at? She still not answering her phone?" Symone asked.

"Yeah, I just hung up with her. She's coming Friday and she gonna show us how to make it so we can do this thing."

"Oh aiight then cuz, I was damn sure ready to go find her and whoop her ass for tryna play us," said Angel.

"Now you sound like Cleo over here," I said laughing. "But nah, she good. Let me see these orders."

"Girl, check out the one for my brother's drug connect. It says Marcello," said Symone.

"Damn, he wants twenty thousand dollars worth?" said Lace, hovering over Jada's shoulder looking at the paper.

"He wants to spend twenty thousand to get forty thousand worth?" Symone said.

"Can we quit now Jada?" Lace asked smiling.

"Yeah, the way this poppin already, I don't think we need to wait a month," said Angel.

"I think y'all right," I said, still looking at the sheets of paper. Let's finish the week out and turn in letters Friday. We don't want to just bounce and they think something happened to us or nuthin'."

"You and that fuckin' CSI," Lace teased. "But okay, cool. Friday and dat's it. We are about to be gettin' too much money to be working a nine-to-five."

Friday Zy came over with two hundred pages of money. She installed all the programs on our computer and spent the remainder of the night teaching us all how to make the money. It wasn't as easy as it looked, but once we had it down we were able to save the images. All we had to do was print and cut from that point on. Angel came up with the idea to order sheets so we could keep track of who wanted what, when and the meeting location and their number. She was always the more business minded one in the group. Leave it to us, all you would have to do was call the cell and we got you. But this allowed us to also keep track of the amount of money that was coming in too so we rolled wit' it. We ran this shit just like a real business.

Before Zy left, she had a stack of order sheets so she could make some deliveries the next day. We gave her most of the locations that were across town where she lived. We split the remainder of the orders amongst ourselves and got the money ready for them.

The weeks and months to follow were ridiculous. The word got out so fast and we had so many orders that we couldn't let muthafuckas tell us where and when no more. All they could say was how much and we gave them a time and place to get it. We couldn't hold out on buying cars no more either, so we hit up the dealers.

"I'm getting a Benz, fa sure," said Lace.

"Yeah, I think I want one too," said Symone.

"I'm getting the new Cadillac truck," I said. "Wait, let me call Zy and see if she wants to meet us there. She is balling now with her new crib and all lat. I know she was saying last week she was getting a new car so I'm a see if she ready."

"I don't know what I want," said Angel. I guess I'll see when we get there."

Zy was wit' it and she picked us up two hours later to go find some cars.

The first dealership we went to didn't want to budge too much on the prices. We told him we would be paying cash and he got excited from the door. He thought just because we had it we were gonna pay when he only took like three thousand off each car. He was wrong. We left that one but it was a lesson learned. We knew not to tell the next mutha- fucka we was paying up front.

The next dealership we went to, we negotiated the sales men down first. Then when we got him to where we wanted him we told him we were paying cash and renegotiated some more. I got a white Cadillac truck like I wanted and Zy got one also in a red color. It was so funny though because Zy was only about five-four, so when she got in for the test drive she looked like a lil ass girl in that big ass truck. But she was driving it like it was nuthin'. They did the paper work and we were out just like that.

We went to the Benz dealer next, Lace got the black CLK, Angel got one in a champagne color and Symone got one in silver. We were riding dead right, but we needed some upgrades early. We went to this spot in Philly called East Coast Customs to get rims, TV's, DVD players, all that. It took all day for them to do the work.

They wanted us to bring the trucks back the next day because they wouldn't have time to do them. We had money to make the next day so we needed all our cars that same day. But damn if money don't talk. We threw them a G extra for each truck and they got it done. We didn't get out of there until like midnight, but it was all worth it. We looked like a car show riding down Route 80. Zy took her exit and beeped the horn to let us know she would holla at us tomorrow. When we got home we went over the orders for the next day and went to bed.

JADA

We had been running the counterfeit money for a year. We had people from different states who bought from us and everything. White, black, Hispanic - it didn't matter. Everybody was buying it. We had this white man that was an executive at some large company who bought fifty thousand dollars worth every month like clockwork. We had another white man who worked in a bank that bought ten thousand dollars worth every week. I don't know what he was doing but I wasn't mad at him. We had hundreds of clients who spent mad dough and hundreds who spent the minimum. We were getting so much money that we had to have four safes installed in the laundry room. One safe for each of us. It was hot how they did it too. They created a floor under the floor for us. The button to make it rise was hidden in the ceiling. It seemed like nothing could go wrong. We got our wakeup call when Zy called Lace all hysterical one day.

Zy pulled up to the high rise projects on Third Street, she hated going there alone. It was one of the worst parts of town in Philly. Rundown apartment buildings lined both sides of the street. A small Spanish owned grocery store sat at the very corner of the street. Across from it were the liquor store and a Chinese restaurant that looked unfit for a dog to eat at. Zy watched the kids running from the corner store eating popsicles. The children looked dirty and un-kept. She thought it was funny how they skipped down the street without a care in the world. Hair uncombed and their clothes looked as if they hadn't been washed since they were bought.

She was taken from her thoughts by the sound of a female's voice yelling to the kids. She turned to find a dark complexioned and very skinny woman standing at the entrance to the projects screaming at them. Her hair and nails looked freshly done. Despite her children's appearance, she seemed to be clean and that made Zy sick.

"Didn't I tell y'all not to leave from in front of the building?"

"We just went to the store mommy."

"I don't give a damn, I told y'all lil asses not to go anywhere. Who gave y'all money for the store?"

"Mike gave us a dollar and said we could share it," said the little girl looking afraid. Her brother lowered the ice pop from his mouth as if he was unsure if it was okay to continue eating it.

"If Mike gave y'all a dollar, why y'all ain't bring it to me? Y'all know I ain't got no cigarettes. I could've gotten me some damn loosies with that. Get y'all bad asses in the house."

Zy watched as they strolled pass one of the buildings that were boarded up. She still didn't see Prince so she called his cell to find out what was up.

"Yeah, who dis'?" He answered on the second ring.

"This Zy. Wass' up? I'm outside."

"Oh aiight. Look, shorty, come to building five right quick. I'm in the middle of something."

"Well how long you gon be?" she asked irritated that he wasn't ready at their scheduled time.

"I'm a be a minute…that's why I'm saying, come to the building and we can handle that."

"Aiight, well meet me in the hallway then," Zy said against her better judgment.

She grabbed the blade she kept in her glove box and the bag that that held the counterfeit money in it. She walked through the projects until she found the building marked five. Before she could even open the door she smelled the strong stench of urine seeping through. She opened the door and almost gagged at the smell. Zy was just about to call out for Prince when a guy appeared from the stairwell on top and grabbed her. Struggling to break free of his grip, she dropped the bag of counterfeit money. She saw Prince jump the small flight of stairs to get it. Still struggling with the guy, Zy removed the knife from her pocket and stuck it in his arm.

"Ahhhh!! Bitch!" he screamed letting her go.

Prince tried to grab her but she was already out the door. They chased her all the way to the car. She only had about a ten second head start on them, so before she could get into the car, they had her again. Zy clawed at their faces with her nails and swung her knife wildly. When she was free of them, she jumped in the truck and tried to close the door. Prince had one foot in and the other hanging out. He grabbed the handle on the side of the truck and tried to pull himself up.

"You want to ride, nigga, then let's ride," said Zy pulling off with him hanging on to the truck.

"Let me off, bitch," Prince screamed trying to get his hands through the small opening in the window to hold on a little better. Zy rolled the window up on his fingers and swerved the truck trying to make him fall off. He continued to scream out in pain. Zy rolled the window down for him to remove his hand. He took that opportunity to jump from the moving truck. Zy watched in her rear view mirror as he crawled up in a fetal position in the middle of the street. He was gripping his hand and holding his leg in obvious pain. She grabbed her phone and called the girls.

"Yo, on some real shit, niggas got me fucked up!" Zy shouted into the phone.

"Yo, what happened?" Lace asked.

"Those mutha-fuckers robbed me! They tried to take my fucking truck too. I stabbed one of 'em and dragged the other one down like half a block. He had one leg in the car and the other one hangin' out."

"Whoa, Whoa. Who robbed you, yo?" Lace asked concerned.

"Those niggas from Third Street." Zy replied angrily.

"Aiight, don't make no more deliveries today. I'm a have Angel take care of it. Don't go home either. Go to a hotel or somethin' and call me back when you get there."

"Aiight." Zy responded in a defeated tone.

Lace flipped her cell to call me.

"Yeah," I answered.

"Where you at?"

"'Bout to make this last run, why Wass' up?" I asked, having no idea at the time, what just went down.

"Nah, don't make no more today. Dem niggas from Third Street just robbed Zy, meet me at the house."

"Word. She aiight?" I asked.

"Yeah, she good, but we chillin' for the rest of the day." Lace told me.

"Aiight, I'll be there in a minute then." I said as I shut my phone and stepped on the gas.

When I pulled up to the house, I saw Angel and Symone's car. I was glad they were home. I told the girls what had went down with Zy and asked Angel to call anyone who didn't get their orders and tell them we would have to reschedule their delivery for the following day.

"Yo, I think it's time we stepped our game up, fa real. Niggas gonna test us every chance they get cuz we females. If we let this shit go, it's only gon' get worse." I said.

"I feel you on that. So what y'all want to do?" said Symone.

"I think we need to get some heat and take it wit' us. We need to be strapped when we make runs from now on. Those muthafuckers who robbed Zy gotta get it fa sure".

"Here you go, another Cleo," said Angel.

"Nah; real talk," I said. "This ain't no game no more. We gettin' too much money out here and niggas startin' to see it. If we don't show them that we not the average chicks and we roll like they roll, then they gonna tear us apart out here."

"Yo, I don't even know how to shoot no gun," said Angel.

"Well, we about to learn fuck dat. I ain't about to go out here and let these mutha fuckers take shit from me," said Symone. I know where a shooting range at too, they'll teach us to shoot."

"Well make that call then cuz, I ain't goin' on no more runs without no heat," I told my girls.

Just then, Lace walked in the door with Zy.

"I thought you were going to a telly," asked Lace.

"I was, until Jada called me after I hung up wit' you. She said to meet y'all here. Yo, I'm so mad I could kill those niggas." Zy said.

"We just might do dat, ma," said Lace.

"I think it's time for us to get some heat," said Lace.

"Dats what I'm talkin' about. We were just sayin dat. But everybody don't know how to shoot so we was gon' go to this spot that Symone know about," I said.

"Well it's still early...y'all want to go tonight?" asked Lace.

"Symone, wass' up? Can we go there tonight?" Lace yelled.

"Nope. He said nobody there to teach us tonight, but we can go tomorrow."

"Ok, well nobody is going out tomorrow by themselves. We gonna pair up and anything that was set for the east side tomorrow, make their ass come to the north side," I said.

The next few days were cool. We made the runs together and every evening we went to practice shooting. Lace was having way too much fun though. I think she's a little trigger-happy for real. One of the guys was trying to sell us some guns they had, but we didn't trust that. We wanted to make sure we got clean guns. One of our regular customers gave us the hook up. His uncle owned a gun shop in Delaware. When he came to pick up his money that week, he brought us some guns to choose from. We bought five, 9-mm's from him since that's what we all were comfortable shooting from our practice.

A week had gone by since Zy was robbed, Lace wouldn't let it go. I don't know if she was just itching to use that gun or if she really wanted to get them niggas for robbing Zy. Either way, she wasn't hearing anything about not handling it.

"Man, I'm telling y'all, we need to get at dem niggas cuz, guaranteed they gon try us again."

"Ok, and when they do, we got somethin' for they ass, but right now we ain't gon trip," I said.

"Fuck dat, I'm a handle it before they get that far," said Lace.

"Anyway," I said, "where are Symone and Angel?

No sooner than I said that, did my cell ring.

"Wass' up, Symone?"

Lace could hear Symone screaming from across the room. She couldn't make out what she was saying, but she knew something had to have happened for her to be so upset.

"You fuckin' kidding me," I said. "Aiight, where y'all at right now? Stay there we on our way," I said and closed the phone.

"What happened, yo?" asked Lace.

"Those mutha fuckers robbed them and Mike tried to rape Angel." I told her, not believing those words were coming out of my mouth.

"I told you!" screamed Lace. "I told you dem niggas was gon' try again. Where Angel and Symone at now? They didn't have the heat on em?" Her voice was hurried and agitated.

"Slow the fuck down, damn. They on Eighteenth Street on the east side, parked on a side street. I told them to stay there. Symone shot at em when she saw them but she missed. That shot gave them enough time to get out the building. But I ain't gon miss, believe dat. Come on."

We jumped into my Escalade and did ninety miles an hour, heading over to the East side to see about our girls.

"Slow down before we get pulled over. We got the hammers on us and shit," said Lace.

I slowed down, but not without sayin' how I was going to kill these mutha fuckers. When we got to Symone and Angel, they told them all the details of what happened.

"Me and Symone been sittin' here thinking of a way to get at them," said Angel. "As much as I wanna just go over there and start blastin' on these niggas we can't do it like that. So this the plan, if they still out there we gon act like we wanna call it a truce and put them down wit' us."

"I don't know, that don't sound too bright. I mean, why would they believe that shit?" I said.

"'Cause we gonna make it look like we are scared. Like we in over our heads or some shit like that. They gonna go for it, trust me." Said Angel.

"Yeah, we'll make it look like we like how they got down, but they can't be tryna do us like dat no more. We'll tell 'em that we can all play for the same team, you know? That we need some men behind us to protect us.," said Symone.

"Still don't sound right." I said.

"It will work." Said Angel.

"I'm with, Jada. Do y'all think they gon' really buy that. And what if they do, then what?" Lace asked.

"Then we tell 'em let's go get a room and talk about it," said Angel."

"Man, I don't know. I don't trust these mutha fuckers at all. I say we just blast they asses and be done wit' it," said Lace.

"Right. What about witnesses and all dat?" I asked. "I don't think this a good idea."

"Aiight, well I got Mike's cell number, so I'ma hit em up and see if they roll wit' it," said Symone."

She called the number but nobody answered. Soon as she hung up the phone rang back.

"Somebody just called Mike from this number?" the caller asked.

"Yeah," said Symone "I wanted to holla at you."

"Yo, who dis?" he asked.

Symone ran the bullshit plan down to them we'd just discussed. And it looked like he was going for it. She put it on speaker so we could all hear him, which confirmed he was all game.

"Yo, I'm feelin' all dat fa real. Y'all need some dudes like us anyway. Sorry it went down the way it did but dats what me and my niggas do, you know? We be tryna eat, but tell ya peoples I ain't mean to try to get it like dat. She just fine as hell," he said laughing.

'It's nuthin', she already said she willin' to over look it if y'all wanna come in wit' us and y'all give y'all word that we all good," said Symone. "We need y'all out here."

"Yo, on everything, y'all bring us in and we all good. And we gon make sure no other niggas fuck wit' y'all either, aiight?"

"Aiight, dats wass' up. So y'all wanna meet us at the Ramada in like a half? We gon' bring y'all some real work and we can talk more there'," said Symone. "Can I trust you?"

"If I give my word, then it's my word."

"Cool."

"Aiight, we gon' see y'all up there den. One." He replied before hanging up the phone.

"Girl, all niggas care about is money and gettin' they dick wet. They dumb as hell," said Angel laughing at the call.

"Why did you tell 'em to meet us at the Ramada?" I asked, "we can't do shit up in there."

"I know, girl, we ain't never gon' make it inside. We gonna get those niggas soon as they pull up. Y'all got them silencers?" said Symone.

"Yeah," I said

"Aiight, come on."

We rode towards the Ramada and parked the cars down the street from it. We knew which direction the dudes would more than likely be coming from and we wanted to make sure we had a clear view of them when they came down the street. So we stood outside hidden behind a few other parked cars.

"Aiight, yo, when we see the car we gon' light they ass up, aiight?" Lace said.

It seemed like forever before the car came but we finally saw the lil gray hoopty Mike drives come down the strip. We caught the light at the corner where we were standing.

Lace yelled out, "Go!" and we all started shooting.

Lace aimed for the tires first so they couldn't pull off. She hit the front and back drivers' side, and then continued to shoot. When we were sure them niggas had to be dead, we got back in our cars and slowly pulled off. We didn't want to make it obvious by speeding off so we cruised. We jumped back on the highway and headed home.

I called Symone and Angel who were riding together.

"Put me on speaker," I said. I waited until I heard an echo and said, "Y'all cool?"

"Yeah...I can't believe we just did that shit," said Angel. "You think they dead, Jada?"

"I don't see why not," I said.

"What if they're not?" said Angel.

"Yo, dem niggas dead for sure. I emptied a clip alone into that car," said Symone.

"Symone, call Mike's cell like twice back to back, leave a message askin' where he at. Tell him you waitin' for him so hit you back as soon as he gets the message," I said.

"What the fuck you talkin' about? Symone said.

"Trust me, just do it." I told her.

Symone flipped her cell and left the message like I told her too. When we all got back to the house we put the burners in their safes, and sat in the living room.

"So why you have me leave that message?" asked Symone.

"Cuz, the last number in that nigga cell might be yours. When they investigate that shit they be calling the last number that called them and the last number that was dialed. So if they contact you for any reason you can say you was suppose to meet him at the Ramada but they never showed up and never returned ya calls. If you had anything to do with it then why would you be calling him after the fact and telling him you waitin' for him, you know? Plus, what if they told somebody they was coming to meet us? All we have to say is they never showed up. Simple as that."

After the conversation, we all stayed home and never went back out. If we all singing the same song, its nuttin' they can do.

"Aiight, Ms. CSI," said Symone. "Damn, I'm hungry. Y'all wanna order a pizza?"

"Yeah that's a good idea too, that way, we can say we was home eatin' pizza and that can be verified with the delivery." I said.

We all laughed.

"You really serious, huh?" said Lace.

"Y'all, bitches laughin', but I bet y'all won't be laughin' lata cuz, I'm right." I told them.

Months turned into two years since we killed Mike and his boy. The media made it out to be some retaliation thing since the two were known for robbing people. They got a few leads, but all turned out to be no good. They did question Symone just like I knew they would - but her story checked out just the way we planned it. We all stuck to the same story so there was nothing they could do. They had no witnesses, no nothing. In the end, no arrests were ever made and it was just another unsolved murder case.

We also took advantage of the opportunity to buy new cars, just in case. I got a Diamond White Aston Martin with all white cashmere leather interior and eighteen-inch D'Vinci chrome rims. Lace bought a Silver Rolls Royce Phantom, grey and white interior with Asanti chrome wheels. Angel bought a candy red Mercedes Benz SLR convertible. The interior is tan premium ash leather and nineteen-inch chrome Diablo rims and tires. Zy snapped with a black M6 BMW convertible. Symone's whip was nice as hell to, she had a Black Mercedes Benz GL 450 beige cashmere leather interior with walnut wood trim. Her twenty-inch Dubs were off the chain.

A while later, Zy was at the car wash getting her truck detailed when Angel called her.

"Wass' up, Angel?"

"Shit. Wass' up wit' you? What you doing?"

"Gettin' my car detailed, girl. Jalen be killin' this car." Zy told her.

"I know what you mean, he had mines looking a mess too last week when we had him," she giggled. "But that's my baby. So, what you getting into lata?"

"I ain't got nuthin' planned and Jalen wit' my mom as usual, so what y'all wanna do?"

"I don't know I wanna get away for a while. I was thinkin' about us takin' a lil vacation. You think ya mom wanna keep Jalen for us for a lil while?"

"You know she will. Since we got her that house and her new car she'll say yes to anything, girl. But you know, that's her baby too so she won't mind. Where y'all wanna go?" Zy asked curiously.

"I don't know. I'ma see what these chicks talkin'. You gon' be home lata? We might come thru." Angel asked.

"Yeah, I'ma be there, so holla at me."

Later, Angel went up stairs to my room. When she opened the door she was in shock by what she saw. She closed it real soft and walked to her room quietly laughing at herself. She thought how glad she was that my eyes were closed because she would've been so embarrassed if I saw her at the time. *'Why she ain't got her damn door locked if she gonna be using vibrators and shit?',* she told me she thought later. It was weird because none of us had a man. We stay so busy making money, a relationship seems non-existent. So I was getting it where I could.

ANGEL IN HER ROOM

I *wonder what it would be like to come home to a man every day.* Angel laid in her bed thinking. She pictured how he would look. Imagined how he would smell like Jean Paul cologne. She thought about the way he would touch her. She imagined kissing him and gently biting on his bottom lip. The next thing she knew her hands began to wander. She pictured him licking on her breasts putting both in his mouth at once. She thought about how he would work his way down licking her inner thighs. He'd get to her clit and slowly lick it. He'd gently suck on it while making circles with his tongue. The more she thought about him the wetter she got. The more she thought about this man the faster her fingers went inside of her. She was ready to climax. She bit her bottom lip as she moaned out in pleasure. Just as she opened her eyes she saw her door close.

A WHILE LATER

After I finished with the dude, I walked to Angel's room. She was taking care of herself. I closed the room door and went back to my room with a smile. I felt guilty for watchin' Angel. I didn't go to her room intending to watch her. I wanted to let her know that I knew she came into my room and I wanted to apologize for not lockin' my door. But when I walked in and saw that I couldn't help but peak through the door. I knew we all probably did it being that no one had a man. Shit what else could we be doing but fuckin' ourselves? I decided I wouldn't say anything to Angel about it. As far as I was concerned we were even so it would be our lil secret.

JADA

We all agreed we wanted to get away. While we were at Zy's house that night we went on the net and made arrangements to spend a week visiting Cali and Vegas. Any new orders that came in we put off for a week. Two days later we were on a flight out.

When we got there, we rented two cars then checked into our hotel suites. After we got settled, we all jumped in the truck and cruised thru Cali for a while to see what it was like. The palm trees were so pretty and the streets were wide out there. Not like the city streets where all the highways had three or four lanes. Only their main strips had three or four lanes. We went shopping on Rodeo Drive, just because. We felt like it was a must that we do that. Lace even went in one of the stores messing with the sales lady, saying how she made a *huge mistake*, like the scene from Pretty Woman. We all laughed so hard. We shopped all day long then went back to the hotel. Symone searched the net to find out the best clubs to go to. We all showered and put on one of the outfits we bought earlier that day. We looked like we were ready for a video shoot.

When we got to the club and saw how long the line to get in was we knew it was time to throw some paper around. No way were we standing in that long ass line. I went over to the bouncer at the door and asked him what the holdup was. He told me that the new rap group *N 2 Deep* was there and they were almost at capacity.

"Well, me and my girls out here on a lil getaway from P.A and it would be a shame not to get in tonight. Maybe you have room for a few more?" I said.

"Look, ma, as fine as you are, I would never tell you no to anything, but I got a long line out here and people been waiting for a minute now." The bouncer told me as he eyed me up and down.

"Well I guess it's too bad that I could care less about that. I'm concerned with me and my girls getting in this club. So maybe you could find a way to make dat happen," I said handing him three hundred dollar bills.

He looked me up and down again and licked his lips before letting us in. We could hear the people on line talking shit.

"They on the guest list, sorry y'all," said the bouncer.

Once we got inside, we went to the bar and ordered some drinks. We could see the VIP area up stairs and a bunch of chicks hanging out with the rappers.

"Wass' up, y'all, wanna go to VIP?" Asked Zy.

"Hell yeah, you think we can get in?" Said Angel.

"Girl, them niggas are all the same. Come on," said Zy as she led the group over to the stairs.

We took our drinks up the roped off stairs where there was a big ass bouncer standing.

"Can I help y'all ladies?"

"Yeah, can you see if the fellas want some better company please?" said Zy in a real sexy and confident voice?

The bouncer looked at all of us and counted.

"Y'all sexy ladies stay right here. Y'all gotta be the finest things in here so I'm sure they won't mind," he said.

He went over and whispered something to one of the rappers and he stood up and looked over at us. He nodded at the bouncer and the guy came over and let us in. When we walked in, the girls in there were hatin' real hard. I guess they knew their five minutes of fame was up. It wasn't long before they were told they could excuse themselves.

They knew it meant that they could beat their damn feet up out of there, so they left sucking their teeth and rolling their eyes.

We chilled with the fellas for the rest of the night sipping on champagne and laughing and joking. We weren't acting like lil groupies like the other chicks and I think they respected us more for that. We told them where we were from and what we doin' there and all that. They kept asking us do we model and all that saying we should get at them sometime, maybe they can put us in one of their videos. We all knew it was a line they probably used all the time. Yeah, we all looked good, but we didn't take the video thing too serious.

Later on when we all were ready to go, they asked us to come back to their hotels with them. I knew our bodies were on fire, but we weren't tryna play ourselves fuckin' these niggas, just cause they're rappers.

"Maybe y'all should see if those chicks y'all kicked out still here," said Symone.

"Oh, y'all gon' do it like dat, huh?"

"Yeah, but thanks for letting us chill with y'all."

"Yo, it's only like one-am, why y'all leaving?"

"We not, I just wanna dance a lil before we go. We'll get at y'all, ok?" I told the rap group and their entourage.

They all looked like they were stuck on stupid. They weren't use to chicks tellin' them no. Normally, the "*I want you to be in our video*" line worked. When we walked down the steps to the dance they stood up and watched us. The girls who were up there with them earlier were still there. He knew he couldn't yell over the music, so he sent the bouncer to get them.

Me and the girls were on the dance floor doin' us when Symone noticed the girls going back up to the VIP room. About an hour later she saw them leaving with the rappers and she couldn't help but laugh. She tapped us and told us to look.

"Y'all see these groupie bitches?" Symone said.

"How you gonna leave wit' some niggas that kicked you out?" asked Angel.

"Girl, they gon' be in a video, they don't care," said Zy laughing.

We all continued to party until our feet hurt. We knew then it was time to go.

We all continued to party in Cali for a few more days. We even got some new clients who told us they had no problem flying out to P.A. to do business with us. They were talking large numbers too. The suit and tie guys wanted the most. It seemed the businessmen were more crooked then the street dudes. We met all types of people in Cali, from different backgrounds but it didn't matter. They all had one thing in common. They wanted to flip counterfeit money somehow.

After we checked out of our suites we headed for Vegas. We set it up so that we could return the rentals at a different location in Vegas. When we arrived, we again checked into our suites and headed straight for the casinos. We had dough to blow and knew we would have so much fun doing it. Zy & I lost about five thousand dollars playing black jack and another three thousand dollars playing roulette. Angel and Symone played slot machines most of the night then headed for the tables later. Symone was up by two thousand dollars when she decided to bet it all. Everyone watched closely as people folded. It was down to me the dealer and another guy. The guy turned his card and had eighteen. The dealer turned his card and had 19. Symone turned her cards and had twenty. Everybody started clapping. It was known that people don't normally win with all the bullshit those dealers do. Symone finally got up after a few more hands and went to play something else. At the end of the night we all had lost about twenty-five thousand dollars in total, but we didn't give a damn. We had a good time.

We went to one of the restaurants and sat and ate dinner. I had the steak, Lace had lobster, Symone and Zy had fish and Angel had chicken. We talked about our lil getaway and how much fun we all were having.

"Yo, I think we need to make it a rule that every three months we go to a different state and chill. I love being away from Philly," said Lace.

"Yeah, I just miss my baby, but other than that I could do this on the regular," said Zy.

We joked about the rappers and the groupies from the club in Cali and talked about all the new business we got before leaving. When we got to the hotel we were so tired and drunk we went to their rooms and passed out.

The next day was just as fun as the day before. During the day we did more shopping, went to a full service spa, and went to this hair salon that all the celebrities bragged about. When they were all done we understood why. They had skills in there. The stylists were talking about some big party going on at this club. It was somebody's birthday and we didn't care whose.

All we heard was all the biggest names in R&B and hip-hop were suppose to be there so we knew we had to go. It was four thousand dollars apiece to get in if you didn't have an invitation, so they were all complaining. We got the name of the spot and found out where it was at and were out.

That night we all dressed to kill. We even made jokes about fuckin somebody tonight.

"What happens in Vegas stays in Vegas." We said in unison.

When we pulled up to the party we saw limo's everywhere. We couldn't wait to see who was in there. The Valet parked our car and we went to the front like everyone else.

"Names?" The guy out front said, looking on some clipboard he had.

"We're not on the list," said Angel.

"Do you have an invitation, ladies?"

"No, we don't," I told the man again.

"Okay, it is four thousand dollars, per person to get in. Y'all can go over there and see the lady in front."

We walked over to the lady taking payments and Lace handed her an envelope with twenty thousand dollars in it. After she counted it, she put a clear band around our wrists. I noticed other people had different colored wristbands.

"Why is every ones wrist band different colors?" I asked.

"Well, the red ones are invited guests so they can get into the VIP rooms. The yellow bands are on the guest list but don't have the invitation itself, it lets us know that their drinks are also all inclusive. And the clear ones are people who paid the fee to get in," she said.

"Damn, all that just for a party?" Lace asked.

"It don't matter, girl, we good anyway. Come on," said Zy.

When we got inside, we saw just how star studded it was. Everyone was there. Actors and actresses, singers, rappers, boxers and basketball players. It was the truth in there.

We went to the bar and recognized a few sports figures sitting there. They started running their lil pick up lines as soon as they saw us. They even refused to let us pay for our own drinks.

"Bartender, whatever they drinking tonight, put it on my bill, okay? All night."

"That won't be necessary," I told them graciously.

"Nah, ma, I insist. My name's Darnell Taylor, I play for the Heat." He said as he then went around and introduced the other two guys sitting with him.

"So what? Y'all some models or actresses?" The football player asked us.

"Neither," I said. "We run our own business out in P.A."

"Really? What type of business?" he asked.

"We manufacture, market, and distribute renditions of different products. We're just out here on a lil vacation, you know?"

The girls turned their heads and looked at me with a look that said "*Daaamn.*" They wanted to laugh so badly but knew that they couldn't.

"Oh okay. Y'all doing y'all own thing, huh," said Darnell, with a big smile on his face.

"Listen, we have a table in VIP if y'all ladies wanna join us," said the other football player while eyeing the hell out of Angel.

"Well, if y'all don't mind, maybe we can take y'all up on that offer a little later tonight?" I asked.

"Yeah, that's cool, whenever y'all ready." He answered almost sadly.

"Thanks for the drinks and we'll see y'all in a bit," I said.

We walked off and made our way through the club.

"Why you ain't wanna go to VIP?" asked Angel.

"We gonna go, just not right now. All these stars in here, I wanna chill for a bit. We gonna get with them in a lil while."

"Yeah you right," said Zy. "I need to find me somebody to get some from," she laughed.

"Girl, we all do," I said.

We mingled with everybody and met some of the biggest stars. We took lots of pictures. We had so many offers to come chill in VIP, that we didn't know which room to go to first. We also had so many cards from people and received a lot of offers to come out to different events. We felt like celebrities ourselves.

When we were done meeting people we headed to check on the baller's like we said they would. We chilled with them for the rest of the evening drinking and talking. We knew that the ball players could have chilled with the real celebrity females if they wanted to, but they seemed content with me and my girls.

At the end of the night, when the guys asked if we wanted to come back to their hotel with them, we told them no. We had already planned on having them come back to the hotel with us though.

"Well," I said with my eyes real low and sexy from feelin' the drinks. "We won't come with y'all but y'all can come with us."

Angel and the football player were in their own lil world. Zy and Lace were ready to take off their panties right there for the guys they were with.

"Oh aiight, well that's cool. Let me go settle the tab and we can go," said Darnell.

"Ok, well you do that, I need to run to the ladies room so I'll meet you downstairs," I said.

"Me too, I'll go with you," said Symone.

They all followed suit and we went to the bathroom, and the guys went downstairs.

"I can't believe we are about to do this," said Zy.

"Fuck that, I can," I told my girls. "This ain't about them and what they want. It's about what I need so I hope this nigga got something to work with," I laughed.

"I know girl, me too. They fine as hell, but if the dick garbage, I'ma be so mad," said Angel.

We left out the bathroom and met the guys downstairs to leave. They had the valets get their cars and the guys followed us back to our hotel. Once we got there we paired off into our suites.

The guys left about ten am that morning. We all were so tired we slept well into the afternoon. When we finally did get up, we all went into Zy's room and ordered up some room service. We were starving but didn't feel like going out.

We ate and exchanged stories about whose dick was big or small. Who had the best head game, which couldn't eat pussy to save their lives, but had a mean pipe stroke. Who took their time and who acted like it was the last time they would ever get pussy again. We talked about who gave the niggas head and who didn't. We made jokes about the faces the guys made while we was riding them and what they sounded like when they was about to bust. When it was said and done we all were pretty satisfied with the fact that we came more than once or twice so we were good.

We spent the remainder of the afternoon chillin at the hotel. We went swimming in their indoor pool and sat in the steam room to relax. We went to a different casino that night and gambled and drank for the rest of the night. It was our last night in Vegas so we took lots of pictures to go with the ones we already had from Cali. When we couldn't drink anymore and we got tired of losing, we went back to the hotel to prepare for our trip home. When we went into our suites, there were two-dozen roses in each room. We all called each other to confirm that we all had them.

"Yeah, girl, they probably do that shit all the time," I said as we all laughed.

The same thing was going on in everybody suites. After we showered, we laid in the bed thinking about how much fun we had and how much drama we would return to in P.A. But, that's the business.

JADA

It's been about seven months since we took that trip and that was one of the best things we could've done. We went out there intending to just get away and have some fun but it proved to be great for business too. Those connections we made gave us a whole new arena of clientele. Once the word was spread in Cali about the counterfeit money in P.A., people were going crazy for it.

We had so many orders to fill, we had to contact the manufacturer of the paper we used and ordered direct from them. We bought five more printers too and had to set the computers to print to all of them so we could save time. It was crazy and we were busy all the time, but the money was rollin' in non- stop so it was worth it. One thing was clear though. The more money we made the more problems we had. Like the day some thirsty ass muthafucka followed me after I made a run.

"Hello?"

"Lace, it's me. Where y'all at?" I asked.

"Umm, Symone on her way back from the airport, Zy and Angel somewhere on the north side and I'm on my way back to the house. Why, wass' up?" Lace asked.

"Somebody is following me," I told her. "I was on my way back to the house and I think dats what he was waitin' for. I'ma stall him and drive around for a while, come meet me by the Walgreens, okay?" I asked her, paranoid as hell.

"Aiight, I'm on my way now." Lace said with her voice full of concern.

I pulled into the Walgreens parking lot and acted like I was looking through my purse for something. I saw Lace's car pull in and called her to tell her where I was parked and told her where the guy in the car was. Lace parked her car a row away from mine and we both got out. I walked towards the store entrance to throw the guy off while Lace crept around to the guys' car. She opened the drivers' side door real fast, and put her nine in his face. I ran over there and we made him get out.

"Get the fuck out the car, if you breathe wrong, I'ma blow you a new asshole mutha- fucka," said Lace.

I took his keys out of the ignition and we walked him to my truck.

"Why the fuck you following me, huh?" I asked. "Get the fuck in the truck."

Lace got in the back with the guy, with her gun pointed at his head the whole time.

"Why the fuck are you following her?" Lace asked him with the gun now pointed in his side.

"I... I.... don't know. I wasn't planning on doing nuthin' I swear," he said stuttering.

"Yeah, okay. You wasn't gonna do nuthin', huh? You lying-mutha-fucker," said Lace hitting the guy in the head with the butt of the gun.

"Chill, yo! I don't need that nigga blood in my car," I told her.

"Well hurry up and get to where you goin' before I kill this nigga right here." Lace said.

"Please, please begged the man. I swear I wasn't going to do anything. They just told me to find out where she lived, that's it. I'll tell you everything, just please let me go." The man pleaded with us.

"Who the fuck is they?" I asked.

"Sammy and Ronnie from New York. They set it up for me to buy the counterfeit money from you so I could follow you and find out where you lived. They wanna rob the place," he said. "I swear it wasn't me and I wasn't gonna do anything. Please, I have a family. Just let me go home to my family." He begged like a lil bitch.

I pulled into a vacant lot on a quiet back road.

"Get out my fuckin car," I said with my gun on him now.

"Please, I beg you. Don't do this. I will tell you how to reach Sammy. I'll do anything you want just please let me go."

"Ok. You wanna live? Call Sammy and give him this address," said Lace.

She went in my truck and wrote something down on a piece of paper.

"Tell him that's the address. When do they plan on coming and don't lie mutha-fucker?"

"Tonight. They were comin' tonight. They're over at a hotel not too far from where I met you. I swear it's the truth. They said at four-am they was gonna be there."

"Okay, get him on the phone," Lace told him.

Lace threw him his cell phone that she took out of his car.

"Yeah it's me. I got it," he read him the address off the paper and hung up.

"Ok, I did it, now please let me go home to my family," the man begged.

"You should've thought about ya family before you decided to fuck wit' us," I said.

I looked over at Lace and gave her a nod, Lace shot the guy in his head close range.

"We gon' leave him out here?" Lace asked looking down at the guy.

"Nah," I said, while picking up the gun casing off the ground.

I got my phone out of the truck and called Symone.

"Yo, I got a problem. I need a big mess cleaned up. You got any ideas?"

"Damn, what happened?" said Symone.

"I'll explain lata, but right now, I need this messed cleaned up."

"Aiight, where you at?"

I told her where we were and she said to just leave dude there. We got in the truck and headed back to Walgreens. Lace got her car and we drove to the house to park it. Then, we went back to Walgreens and Lace got the guys car. I made her take it to the car wash before we took it back to where we killed the guy at. The body was already gone when we got there. We took all the paper work out the car and removed the license plates. We set the car on fire and left it there to burn.

When we got back to the house Lace and I took all our clothes off, even our panties and bra's.

"Yo, why the fuck we doing this again?" Lace asked.

"Cuz, I don't want shit we had on in this house, that's why. Just give me ya stuff," I said.

Lace handed me the clothes and shoes and I threw everything in the fireplace.

"Give me those earring's too."

"Oh hell naw, I just bought these! You don't just burn five-carat diamond princess cut studs, Jada. You takin' this shit too far," said Lace.

"You shot that nigga at close range and blood could've splattered. Give em here. Go buy some more, damn." I responded, irritated that she was tripping over something materialistic.

"Ain't no fuckin' blood on my earrings," said Lace, examining the earrings. "But here, if it'll make you feel better, burn em. Damn. Thirty thousand dollars down the drain."

"It will, so thank you. Let me find out you whining about a punk ass thirty grand," I said while throwing them into the fire.

"I could've gotten them cleaned you know," said Lace walking off.

After everyone was brought up to speed on what happened that day, we figured out what we were gonna do about the dudes coming at four in the morning.

"I gave 'em Zy mother's old address," said Lace.

"So, we goin' there or what?" Angel asked.

"Yeah, it's one o'clock now, so we can head out at like two-thirty," said Zy.

We loaded our guns and just chilled until it was time to go.

Lace parked the car across the street from the house and turned off the lights. Nestled in her hip was a .22 caliber, comfortably sitting like it was a part of her. We put the silencers on the 9mm's and sat waiting for the men who we thought were going to rob us to get there. When they finally showed up at quarter-to-four in the morning, we watched them as they drove slowly down the street looking for the house. When they found it, they parked the car and two men got out. They even had the nerve to be wearing masks. We all got out the car real quietly and crept up behind them.

"Pssssss." Angel said real soft to get their attention. As soon as one of the men turned around, Lace raised the nine and set the tip of the silencer from the gun against the side of his head. Angel let three quiet rounds spray at one of the other guys. His partner watched helplessly as his lifeless body lay on the ground.

"Which one are you, Sammy or Ronnie?" I asked with my gun directly on his atoms apple.

"I'm Ronnie," he mumbled.

Angel walked around to the left side of him and snatched the mask off his face.

"I want you to get a good look at us muthafucka," she said.

Ronnie took a deep breath as he looked into the eyes of each of us. His last breath came when he turned to me. Just as he thought how it could be possible to be that beautiful and hard at the same time, I squeezed the trigger. When he fell to the ground, Lace and Angel dumped four more shots in him.

We went back to the car and Symone made a call.

"Yeah, come on," is all she said and hung up.

We looked up and saw a van pull up and two guys jumped out. Lace drew her gun but Symone told her it was cool. They picked up the bodies and put them in the van. They took out some containers and poured something where the blood was and scrubbed it up with a push broom. They poured what appeared to be water over it and repeated the same steps about three times before getting back in the van and leaving.

"Ladies, our new clean-up crew," said Symone.

"Why you ain't tell us they was here?" asked Lace. "You almost got the clean-up crew killed."

"Who are they and where they takin' the bodies?" I asked.

"The same place they took ole boy earlier," said Symone. "But don't worry, Ms. CSI, they never gonna be found where they going, so don't worry about it, okay?"

"Bitch, you crazy, you know dat?" said Lace. "Come on let's go."

"Damn, wait a minute. Help me find the shells," I said.

I took some flashlights out the truck and found the casings and left. When we got to the house, I burned the sweat suits and everything we wore.

"Dats why I told y'all to make sure y'all didn't wear no good shit and definitely no jewelry," said Lace sarcastically.

We all laughed.

JADA

A year later we were knee deep in money. Our business was still going strong but we had a huge problem. The media now had wind of counterfeit money going around. Large and small businesses were complaining, fast food chains, clothing stores, everyone put it in complain't s. The news urged retailers to check bills from customers. It wasn't killing our clientele yet, but we were worried that it would.

Not only that, if somebody got caught with it, we was worried that they would tell where they got it from. That's when I received a life changing phone call. I hadn't spoken to my aunt and uncle in years so I was shocked when my uncle left a message on my cell phone.

"Jada, this is ya Uncle Frank. I've been trying to get in contact with you for a long time," he said in his accent. "There is someone very important who would like to speak with you. Please call him at 555-846-2145. His name is Rubin and he will explain everything then. Also please call and let us know how you're doing. Bye."

What the hell could he possibly want? I thought. Now he cares about how I'm doing? I ain't calling him back, but I would like to know who this Rubin dude is. My uncle is so shady he might be a Fed. I dialed the number my uncle left and what sounded like an old man answered.

"Yeah?" He said coughing into the phone.

"Can I speak to Rubin?"

"Yeah this is me, who wants to know?" The hoarse voice said into the phone.

"My name is Jada. I was told that you wanted to speak wit' me about sumthin."

"Jada? Oh yeah. You're Ricardo's little girl. Yes?"

"You knew my father?"

"Yes. Yes. Very well, actually. We worked together for many years."

"Well my dad has been gone for a long time, so what do you want with me?"

"Yes, I know, Jada. And I'm terribly sorry about your loss. I know you're much older now, and it's a bit late, but I am very sorry. Ricky was a good man and a great friend to me."

"Well thank you, but if that's all you needed, I'm kind of late for an appointment."

"Well there are some things I wanted to discuss with you. But I'm not one for long conversations by phone. Maybe you will meet with me. Yes?"

"Look," I replied, "I appreciate you taking the time to offer your condolences about my father, but I don't know about meeting you. I don't even know you."

"Yes, this is true, Ms. Jada," he said in his heavy accent. "But there are many things I would like to discuss with you. You can bring your friends if you like."

"What? My friends?" I asked.

"Yes, your friends. You make the money with them. Yes?"

"I don't know what you're talking about and I have to go." I said quickly.

"Wait, Ms. Jada. I do not mean to upset you. As I said, your father was a great friend and I will forever be in debt to him for all he has done. I will not upset you further but I must speak with you but not on the telephone. You take this address. Yes?"

He gave me the address and told me to come there tomorrow at noon. I agreed to be there and hung up.

I decided not to tell the girls about my meeting with Rubin just yet. I wanted to see what he wanted first. I didn't feel threatened by him or in danger so I went alone. When I got there I pulled up to the gate and buzzed the button. I thought about how much it looked like a scene from a movie and had to laugh at myself. *Rubin sure was livin' large,* I thought.

"Welcome, Jada, please come through," said a woman's voice through the speaker.

How the hell she know my name? I thought. I pulled around the long circular driveway and got out the truck. A woman stood in the door in a maid's uniform and let me in.

"Please follow me." She said as she led me down the foyer.

She took me to a large room where a man sat in a chair smoking a cigar. He looked to be about sixty years old. I knew that had to be Rubin.

"Hello, Ms. Jada. Welcome to my home. I see you decided not to bring your friends."

"No I didn't."

"Well perhaps next time. Yes? You are very beautiful girl, Jada. And you have done well for yourself. Your father would be very proud man." He told me in his broken English.

"Thank you. But how do you know about what I do? You said yesterday me and my friends make money?"

"Yes, there is not much that happens here that I don't know about, Ms. Jada."

"Well, if you can find out, then anybody can find out and that bothers me."

"Let me tell you this. I find out things the police will never know of. So please, do not be alarmed. You and your friends are in no harm. I would know if the police knew who made the money and they do not."

The maid came in with a big bowl of fruit and some juice on a tray that she sat on the table in front of us.

"Please…help yourself, Ms. Jada."

I poured a glass of juice and continued to listen.

"So exactly why did you want to meet me? Do you want in on my business or somethin'?"

Rubin laughed and then began to cough real hard.

"For heaven's sake, no. I do not "want in" as you call it. I wanted to meet with you to let you know that if you ever need anything from me, I will be here. You just let me know. As I said, your father and I were friends and there is something I never got to repay him for. I will do that by helping out his only child anyway that I can."

"Thank you for the offer, but you already know, I do pretty well for myself so I'm good."

"Jada, do you know what your dad did for a living?"

"Yes, I found out a few years after him and my mom was killed. I assume that's what you do also?"

"Well again. If there is anything I can ever do, no matter how big or small, please call on me."

"There is one thing you can do for me," I said seeing this as an opportunity to open a new door. "I want in the game. But not small time. I want it all."

"I see. I have been retired for many years now, Ms. Jada. But, if that is what you wish to do, you must know that it's much different from what you and your friends do now."

"I know that, we can handle it." I replied.

"I see. Tell me, Ms. Jada, what do you mean when you say you want it all?"

"I mean, I want to be able to supply as many states as I can."

"I see. As I said, I am a retired man so I cannot play the middle. You will need to run the show yourself. I'm sure you will be fine. You are just like your father. Very strong. I will make some calls, Jada, and call you in a few days. Yes?"

"Yes. Thank you, Rubin," I said standing to leave.

"My pleasure, Ms. Jada. Thank you for coming today and I will speak to you soon."

When I got in my truck I wanted to scream. I had been looking for a way to get in the drug game. Only Rubin could get me in at the level I wanted to play at. I knew it was much more dangerous but I would make sure me and my girls were ready for war when the time came. I rode the rest of the way in deep thought about what could be in store for us. I decided to wait and see what happened before I told the girls anything.

A week had gone by since I met with Rubin. I was at the house getting orders ready when my cell phone rang. I got excited as soon as I saw his name and number appear.

"Hello." I answered."

"Hello, Ms. Jada. How are you?"

"I'm fine thank you, and you?" I asked politely.

"Well, I am as well as I can be. I have taken care of what you wanted. You come to my home again and I will give you all the details. Yes?"

"Yes I can come. When?" I asked.

"You will come now. Yes?"

"Yeah I can come now, I'll be there in a few, okay?"

"Ok, I will see you then, Jada."

I put everything away and headed straight to Rubin's house. When I got there I saw a big U-Haul truck parked outside with three guys standing by it. I buzzed the buzzer and the maid let me in.

"Good afternoon, Jada."

"Good afternoon." I replied.

She brought me back to that same room as before, where Rubin was waiting.

"Hello again, Ms. Jada."

"Nice to see you," I replied.

"I'm afraid we do not have much time, so I will be quick. The guys out front have to be going soon. I made a few calls and was able to get you what you wanted to start off with. You will owe no one anything for this first shipment. This was done as a favor to me and your father. Here is the information you need to continue further," he said handing me a sheet of paper. "He will speak with you and only you. It will then be your responsibility to get your product here to P.A. He will provide several options for you and tell you the cost. But again he will only deal with you, okay?"

"Ok, that's fine. Thank you, Rubin. I really appreciate what you've done for me."

"It is with great pleasure, Ms. Jada that I assist you. You will be safe. Yes?"

"Yes I'll make sure we're safe." I answered.

"Ok then. The guys out front will follow you to your home. I know you don't let people know where you live. But they are from me okay? No harm will come to you from them. They will not even speak much under my order okay."

"How do you know I don't like people knowing where I live?"

"Your uncle told me you never told him where you lived. Your father was much the same way, so it did not surprise me at all," he laughed. Then let out a cough.

"Thanks again, I will be in touch Rubin, okay."

"Okay, Ms. Jada. Goodbye."

I headed home with the guys in the U-Haul in tow. When they got there they barely even spoke to me just like Rubin said. All they wanted to know is where I wanted the stuff. When they opened the U-haul door I almost fell to my knees. I didn't know exactly how much was there, the truck was damn near full from front to back and top to bottom. I had them stack everything neatly in the great room. After they left I sat on the sofa and stared at it for the remainder of the day. When the girls got home and asked me what was all that, I simply responded.

"Our new business."

JADA

I told the girls all about Rubin and how we came up on the coke. They were just as shocked as I was about how much we had.

"Yo, and he just gave you this for free?" asked Lace. "This is millions of dollars worth of shit. It gotta be on some consignment type of shit."

"Nah, I told y'all. This is all free. The next time we get some, we have to pay."

"I can't believe this," said Angel. "How we gon' move all this weight?"

"The same way we moved the money," said Symone.

"Yo, niggas gon' be on some dumb shit, for real now. Think they was wildin' over the counterfeit, we about to change the game fa real now," said Lace.

"Well, they either roll wit' it or get ran over cuz I'm tryna get it all out this muthafucka," I said.

Just then, Zy walked in the house with Jalen. After they all took turns hugging and kissing on him, Angel sat him in front of the T.V. and put on the DVD that taught him his colors and numbers.

"So, wass' up around here? What y'all have to tell me?" asked Zy.

We brought her up to speed on the drugs then talked about how we would move it.

"I think we should only deal with large weight. I ain't tryna supply the lil local guys. I wanna supply the big boys, you know?" I said.

"Yeah, we have to be competitive with the price if we want to get the clientele. I'll make a few calls and find out what's going on out there," said Symone.

"Aiight cool, I'ma find out who supplies who and where. I have a feeling Rubin might know exactly who the major dealers are," I said.

"Wouldn't that interfere with his business though?" asked Angel.

"Nah, they out the game. He just called in a favor to get us this."

"We gon' have to take a few trips too to put the word out there," I said.

"Yeah, to save time, I think we should pair up and hit up a few states each," said Lace.

"I'm wit' dat," said Symone.

For the next few hours we sat and got all our ideas together. We decided we would still make the counterfeit money too until we got it going with the coke. But once things started flowing, we were going to shut it down for good.

In the weeks to follow, we all did our homework. Rubin actually put us on to a lot more than I thought he would. We now had the names of some of the top dealers and knew where to reach them. We decided that Symone and Lace would go to Delaware, Maryland, D.C and Virginia. The rest of us would handle Jersey thru Connecticut. We went to all the places Rubin told us too and hit up, all the hottest clubs where the major players hung out.

We set up meetings at hotels and restaurants, even a car show in N.Y. We met dealers at big boxing matches in Atlantic City and NBA games. We didn't care where they wanted to meet as long as it was an open environment, we were good with that. We had tester bottles to give out so they could try the product. If they liked it, we arranged for them to come out to Philly and pick it up. We knew we had some of the best coke out there so we sold it for five thousand less per kilo than what the dealer was already paying.

Better coke at a better price, niggas would've been stupid not to buy from us. It took about two weeks for everyone to get back home, but it was well worth the traveling. We had it set up so almost all the top dudes would buy from us.

"Girl, let me tell y'all about these guys in D.C.," said Symone. "Lace and I get to this strip club one of them own. Bitches running around naked and all lat. So we following the bouncer to the back of the club where the dude office at, right. Tell me why when we walk in, this nigga on his cell phone talking, while some bitch givin' him head? Not only that, it was these two chicks on the couch fuckin' each other. Coke laid out all on the table. Girl it was crazy. But dats not the craziest thing about it.

"We wanted to leave and come back and he was like nah, that ain't necessary right. So, we thought he was gon' clear the room. Don't you know this muthafucka continued to get head and watch these chicks eat each other out while we told 'em the deal. After he nutted in her mouth is when he cleared the room. He had us sittin' there talkin' and watchin' the shit." We all burst out into laughter.

"Shit, just be lucky he ain't ask y'all to join," said Zy laughing.

LACE

Lace was making a drop off when our first customer called wanting six kilo's.

"When you wanna get it?" Lace asked.

"I can be there in two days, is that enough time?" he asked.

"Yeah dats cool. You comin' by ya'self right?"

" Nah, I wasn't. Is that a problem for you?" he said.

" How many people gon' be wit' you? I just need to make sure I'm good, feel me?"

"It's two of us," he replied.

"Aight, call me when you ready," said Lace.

I don't trust any of these mutha fuckers, Lace thought to herself. I don't have no problem making niggas organ donors if I feel anything shady going on. I know this a different ball game and niggas are going to try to be slick because they are dealing with females. If they think for one second they can sleep on us, they gon be deadly mistaken. Let em try.

Zy was rushing to get in the house. She had Jalen in one arm and was fumbling for her key with the other when her phone rang.

Damn I'm going to pee on my fuckin' self if I don't get in here.

She got the door open and put Jalen down. She ran to the bathroom and made it just in time to avoid a mess. She grabbed her cell out her purse and answered it.

"Hello?"

"Yeah, let me speak with Nicole."

Zy knew it was somebody wantin' coke cuz that's who she told them to ask for.

"Yeah, this me, wass' up?"

"This is Carlos, from Brooklyn." He replied.

"Okay, wass' up Carlos from Brooklyn, you need sumthin?"

"Yeah I want ten. When can I get dat?"

"As soon as you come to P.A., when can I expect you?"

"What you ready now?"

"I'm always ready." she answered.

"Ok, I'll be there tomorrow then."

"Call me when you get here and I'll tell you where to meet me, okay?"

"Aiight." Carlos said as he hung up the phone.

Zy cleaned herself up and went to take off Jalen's coat. She fixed him something to eat and let him run around while she got her orders ready for the next day. Zy really wasn't feelin the whole drug game thing. She didn't want to let the girls know for fear that they would think she wasn't loyal. But the fact was she knew how heavy the game could get. It wasn't like selling counterfeit money.

She saw how they had to kill niggas over that and knew that with drugs involved it would be ten times worse. She was sitting on a couple mill and that's all she felt she needed.

Zy watched Jalen as he played with his toy truck making zoom sounds as he rolled it on the floor. She looked at him with his curly hair and innocent brown eyes. She thought of what would become of him if she got caught up in the game. She would either continue to kill or be killed. If she was lucky she would end up in jail. Those were the only options she saw.

It would be just a matter of time when the streets caught up to them and she didn't know of any hood tales where the millions were spent on living out the rest of their days in luxury. She wasn't taking the chance of losing her son or Jalen losing his mother. Nothing was more important than him. She knew it might upset the girls if she was out. Especially now, she was sure they needed her. She was grateful for all that they have done for her and Jalen but she accomplished what she set out to do and that was make a better quality of living for her and her baby. With over three-point-five million in her safe she was more than okay. She decided she would help them out for a while and that was it. She could only hope they would understand and they all could remain friends.

JADA

I was asleep when my phone rang at quarter to four in the morning. I picked up my cell and answered with an annoyed voice.

"Hello?"

"Yeah, can I speak to Jada?"

"This Jada, who dis?" I angrily replied.

"This Juan, from Connecticut," he said sounding wide-awake.

"Do you know what time it is?"

"Yeah, it's business hours, so you doin' business or what?"

"What you want?"

"I need ten. Can I get it by Wednesday?"

"Yeah, call me when you close and we'll meet okay?"

"Okay."

"And, Juan, don't make your business hours my problem again. Understood?"

He laughed. "Yeah, I get it, mami. You're a tough one, huh? I like dat."

I didn't even respond, I just hung up the phone.

Zy told Carlos to meet her at a Spanish restaurant not far from the hotel she got a room at. When she got there, Carlos and his guy were already there and were eating.

"Hey, Nicole, hope you don't mind us eating. We were starving over here. Dis my partner, Styles."

"No that's fine."

"Where's the money?"

"Right here," said Carlos pointing to a briefcase on the floor.

"Good," she said picking it up. "I need to go count the money anyway. Y'all stay here and eat and I'll be back, okay?"

"Whoa, whoa. You not goin' nowhere by ya'self," said Styles.

"Either I go alone or y'all just drove out here for nuthin'. Dis how I work. Take it or leave it."

"Chill, Styles. I don't think Nicole is ready to die yet, right, Nicole?"

"Whatever, muthafucka. Try me if you want to and that rice and beans will be the last meal you ever have. I'll be back in a half hour."

Zy went to the hotel where Lace was waiting for her. They counted the money and it was a million flat. Zy put the ten keys in their briefcase and headed back to the restaurant. They were standing out front smoking a cig when she pulled up.

"You all good, Nicole?" Carlos asked.

"Yeah, we good. Here you go. See y'all next time." She handed them the work.

"Whoa, whoa. We need to check this and weigh it. I'll go inside in the bathroom and do it," said Styles. "Stay put."

While Styles checked the work Carlos made an attempt to make small talk with Zy.

"So, Nicole, what's a beautiful girl like you doin' out here in these streets?"

"Being beautiful doesn't keep me lavish, that's what."

"Well, I don't know who you got for a man, but I damn sure wouldn't have a woman as beautiful as you out here doin' this. I can keep you lavish just like you want. Wass' up?"

"Ain't a damn thing up. Strictly business and nuttin more." Zy answered.

"Are you always so cold and feisty? See, you need a good man to keep you smiling."

"Well that may be true, but either way you're not the man for the job, so let it go."

Styles came back and nodded at Carlos to indicate they were good.

"Well maybe next time I see you, you'll be in a better mood. See you next time, Nicole."

"Later y'all."

Zy headed back to the Hotel. Lace already took the money to the house and was on her way back to the room. They still had customers coming to get money so they used the room all day until the orders were done.

JADA

We've been at the game for just over a year now. We found out that the largest orders didn't come as fast or as often as we thought it would. So, we started selling to smaller dealers too. We still didn't supply the lil nickel and dime boys but we did sell it by the pound instead of just keys. That money came like clockwork. Everything was going good until some niggas from N.Y. came up wanting twenty pounds.

Symone and I were at the hotel waiting for them to call when they got to the meetin' spot. Symone didn't trust these niggas from the door. They were real nervous sounding on the phone and kept saying shit like, "It's only two of y'all right?"

"Yo, I ain't feelin these niggas, fa real."

"I know me either," I told her. "Instead of meeting them somewhere else, let's bring 'em here. I got an idea."

"You sure about this?"

"Trust me."

Symone waited for them to call back and told them to come to the hotel. She gave them the room number and told them to come upstairs one at a time. They weren't feelin that and it made me and Symone even more suspicious. It was our coke so it should've been our rules. The more they went against us, the more uncomfortable I was.

"If y'all don't want to do it like that then it's nuttin'," said Symone.

"Why you want us to come separate? It don't add up."

"We want to make sure ya'll on the up and up. If you don't trust us it don't make us no mind. So what you want to do? We don't have a lot of time for this shit."

They finally agreed to come up one at a time and I went in the hall and watched them as they made their way to the room. When I saw it was only one, I waited for him to walk past me and crept behind him with my gun.

"Yo! Go to the room and don't make a fuckin' sound. If you say a word, I'ma put one through that fitted you got on! Go head!"

I took him in the room and Symone searched him. He had two guns on him. She took them and emptied the clips. She put the guns in the drawer and made him sit on the bed. Symone called for the other guy to come up. We repeated the same steps until all three guys were in the room.

"Tell me why the fuck y'all three niggas got six guns, but no money to pay for twenty pounds?" Symone asked.

"The money is in the car. Word is bond, we thought y'all was gon try some shit like dis so we ain't bring it up."

"Bullshit muthafucka! How about y'all niggas thought cuz we was females y'all could rob us," I said.

"Nah! We wasn't try'na rob y'all ma. Real talk. Let me go get the dough out the car so you can see we weren't tryna play y'all."

"You got five minutes to get to the car and back. If you take longer than dat I'ma think you up to no good and shoot ya boy here in his leg. For every minute longer you take, I'ma shoot them in a different spot. So fuck wit' me if you want to," said Symone.

"Aiight, I'll be right back."

He went to the car and I watched his every move without him knowing it. I saw him open the trunk and pull out a lil duffel bag and head back towards the entrance. I went upstairs and watched him as he walked down the hall towards the door. I walked right behind him in case he tried anything slick. When we got back in the room he gave me the bag with the money it.

"Yo! You must be fuckin kidding me right?" I said.

I lifted my gun to his head and threw the bag over to Symone to look in.

"I know y'all niggas ain't serious right? Tell me why I shouldn't blow ya fuckin' head off right now?"

"What man? It's all there. Count it ma!"

Symone hit him in the head with the butt of the gun.

"Muthafucka this money ain't real and I know you know dat!" Symone shouted.

"I told y'all this shit wasn't gonna work," said the one who looked the youngest.

"You know what, take y'all fuckin' clothes off," I said.

"Come on, ma, y'all ain't gotta do it like dat. We were dead wrong. We gon be out and y'all ain't gonna hear from us ever."

"Y'all mutha-fuckers came here to rob us with the counterfeit money we make and now you want a bitch to have some sympathy for you? Strip muthafucka," she said putting the silencer on her gun.

I grabbed the garbage bag out the wastebasket and wrapped it around Symone's gun. Symone looked at me like *what the fuck* but I didn't blink.

"Get on ya knee's," I calmly told them in a menacing voice.

"Please yo, don't do this shit! I swear we gon be out ma! Please! Hellllllllpp!!!" he screamed.

Pop, pop, pop.

Symone shot the other two before they had a chance to open their mouths.

I removed the bag from the gun and the shell casing was in it. I picked up the other two casings from Symone's gun.

"Call the clean up guys while I get this stuff together." I said.

Symone made the call while I gathered all their clothes and the guns and put it all in the duffel bag. They left the key to the room under a vent in the hallway for the guys and left.

"Yo, how they gon' get the bodies out without anybody seeing them?" I asked.

"They said they were coming in an ambulance dressed as E. M. T's." said Symone. "Don't worry. Everything's gonna be fine."

We checked out the hotel in the fake name we used and headed home.

When we got there I did my thing and burned all the clothes. I burned the duffel bag, the counterfeit money the dudes had and their clothes.

"I'm going to take me a hot shower," said Symone as she headed downstairs.

"Yeah, me too. I'll see you in a bit." I said to my girls as I walked to my room.

Later that night, after we told everybody what happened we laughed at how funny it was.

"They had our money in the bag," laughed Symone. "They actually tried to buy work, with the money we make."

Y'all should've blown their heads off wit' out warnin' as soon as y'all saw dat. I wish I was there," said Lace.

"Yeah, I bet," said Symone. "You would've loved to empty a clip out on somebody," she giggled.

The drama didn't end after we killed those niggas from N.Y. It turned out that they bragged to a lot of people that they were coming to rob us. When they didn't come back, we had half of Queens tryna get at us. We told everybody the same thing. Those lil niggas robbed us for twenty pounds and left us in the hotel naked and tied up to the chairs. I guess that wasn't sittin' too good wit' one of the dudes brothers cuz he came to see us himself to cop. He wasn't on any revenge shit though. He really thought his brother was tryna come up on his own, so he and boys took the coke he copped and left. He kept telling us how he thought they might've gone down south and asked if they mentioned anything like that. We told him all they kept sayin' was, 'We gon be out wit' dis son. Dis gon put us on.' He believed everything we told him and apologized for what they did. The funny thing is he gave us the money for half the coke they took and wanted to do business wit' us again later. Shit, I felt kinda bad for taking the extra money but Symone and Lace ain't give a fuck.

"Dem niggas was gon rob us and who knows, we could've been the ones in that room dead. So fuck 'em and fuck his brother too! Fuck they mother for havin' 'em and fuck they kids," said Symone. "I'm tired of these broke ass mutha fuckers thinkin' it's a game cuz we got a pussy and no dick. So every time they try us, they gon get the same results."

"Damn. You mad huh?" I said jokingly.

"What you think?"

"I'm wit' you, but the thing is, we actin' like we the victims. Unless the message is clear that we murdered them, they may try us again."

"They know what it is. And dis shit ain't funny either," Lace jumped in. "This da shit I kept tryna tell y'all before. But it's nuttin'. It's the game and if we wanna play, then we gotta worry about shit like dat. Long as we handle it, we good. Feel me?"

ANGEL AND ZY

Angel was on her way to meet Zy at the hair salon. They didn't have anything to do that day so they planned on hanging out. She was pulling into the parking lot of the salon when Zy saw her through the window. She watched another car pull in after her and could tell something wasn't right. She jumped out the chair and ran outside just as Angel was opening the door. The two guys hopped out their car and drew guns on Angel.

"Bitch, gimmie the keys!!" The first guy shouted.

"And I'll take the purse and jewelry too." The second guy said.

Angel handed one the keys to her Benz and the other dude her purse. She was taking her jewelry off when she saw Zy creeping up from the corner of her eye. She dropped one of her diamond earrings on the ground on purpose so she could bend down.

"Bitch, pick dat shit up!! Hurry the fuck up too!!"

Angel bent down and soon as she did she heard the gunshots. Zy shot one of them in the chest and he dropped the gun. The other dude started shooting back at her then grabbed Angel by her hair and put the gun to her head.

"I'll kill dis bitch!! Drop the fuckin the gun!!" He yelled.

"I ain't dropping shit!! You kill her and I kill you. You can't shoot both of us at the same time muthafucka so make ya choice!!"

"Yo, get in the car!! Open the fuckin door, bitch!!" He yelled to Angel.

Angel opened the car door like he told her too and climbed in. Before he could even close his door good, she opened the passenger side door and got out. He shot at her but missed. He turned the car on and sped off while Zy was still shooting at him. He got away.

"Get the fuck up nigga!" Angel said kicking the other guy on the ground. She had his gun pointed at him.

"Get up!" said Zy.

"Ahhh!" he moaned out in agony as Angel kept kicking him.

"Who the dude you was wit' muthafucka?"

"They call him True," he groaned.

"Where dat nigga be at? Answer me muthafucka, you ain't dead yet!!"

"He hangs out on South Street," the man replied in between moans.

Angel shot him in his head, and her and Zy walked off.

"Wait! The casings. If we leave these here Jada will have a fit. Help me find them," said Angel.

Angel and Zy picked up the shell casings like Jada always did before they walked off. They went to the salon where the couple of people who was in there was at the door watching.

"Y'all ain't see none of this shit right?" Zy said handing everybody a wad of cash. Angel followed suit and handed each of them another wad.

"We ain't see a damn thing," they all said.

"Aiight. Somebody is going to be here in a lil while to clean that nigga up, I'll call you to come do my hair instead of coming to the salon," Zy told the owner of the salon.

They got in Zy's truck and pulled off. Angel called Symone to have the clean-up crew handle the guy in the parking lot.

When they got to Zy's house they called Lace and Jada and told them what happened.

"Damn! We just talked about this shit," said Lace! "I'm ready to put all these broke ass niggas in one house and blow it the fuck up," she screamed. "So who got ya car?"

"Some nigga named True."

"Aiight, he got that for now. We gon' wait a while before we see about him. Too much shit happening right now. So, let's wait like a couple of weeks then go find him."

"Aiight cool. I'll see y'all in a lil while."

On the way back to the house Angel pulled off on the highway and threw the dudes gun in the river. They burned all their clothes like Jada always did, showered and chilled until everybody else got there.

JADA

It took us three months to catch up to True. The insurance company already paid Angel for the car and she got a new one by then but, dat nigga still was gon' get what he had comin' to him. We found him at an afterhours spot in South Philly bragging about how he gettin' money out here.

"Y'all, niggas ain't hittin' like I'm hittin'," he said taking another sip of his drink before rolling the dice in his hands. "Dats why these hoes love me and give me more ass than a toilet get. They know how I get down." He was talking real loud and reckless and niggas already wanted to pop him in there.

"Nigga, roll the damn dice," said a thugged out looking young guy, obviously annoyed with True.

"Breathe, nigga, damn. Don't be in such a rush for me to take ya dough, nigga."

"Man, we suppose to be shootin' craps and you shootin' off at the mouth like a nigga won't bless you in here," the young thug said gripping the steal under his white tee.

"Nigga, you reaching for what," said True drawing out his own piece.

"Hey now, hey" said the bartender. "We ain't having all that in here tonight. Y'all niggas gotta go."

"I'm about to go anyway," said the young thug. "This nigga is trippin'."

He picked up his money off the floor and headed for the door.

"Yeah, I bet you are leaving nigga. You don't want any problems wit' True. Hey my, nigga, let me get another shot, double shot of Henney and I'ma be out too."

True threw back the double then headed for the door.

We waited all night until he left the bar and followed him to the run down building he was living in. He was drunk as hell and swerving all through the streets in the lil Honda Accord he was driving. We parked the car and watched as he got out stumbling all the way to the entrance. When he got to his door, Lace rushed him and hit him with the barrel of the gun. I took his keys out his hand and opened the door to the apartment. We pushed him in the house and closed the door.

"Bitch, ya car gone so I don't know what the fuck you want!! I already told the cops y'all killed my boy, so y'all goin' down," he laughed.

I hit him in his mouth with my gun.

"Shut the fuck up! What you do with the car?"

"I took it to the chop shop, baby. The chop shop, baaaby." He sung the words like it was a song and laughed.

Angel kicked him in his balls and he let out a loud scream.

"Get me a chair. I got somethin' for dis nigga," said Lace. "Take ya clothes off mutha fucka! You been braggin' about ya dick all night, let me see what you workin' wit'."

"Oh y'all need some dick? Dats why y'all ran down on me?" He laughed. "Dats all you had to say. Who wanna get piped first?"

"You think this a game nigga? Take ya clothes off," said Lace, cocking her gun.

He stripped down to his under wear and socks.

"Nah, dude, take everything off," said Angel.

He took off his boxers and we all laughed at how small his dick was. Lace snatched the cords from the phone wires and tied his arms to the chair. Then she tied his legs with the cords from his play station game.

"We gon' have a lil fun wit' you, nigga, since you wanna rob chicks, steal cars, bust guns and all lat," said Angel.

Zy looked in the bathroom and found a bottle of bleach under the sink.

"Open ya mouth, nigga! You been talkin' slick all night. Open ya fuckin' mouth!!"

Lace and I pried his mouth open and Angel poured the bleach down his throat. He tried his hardest not to swallow and spit it out but it was nothing he could do. He started gagging and screaming.

"Don't scream now, muthafucka," Zy said.

She lit one of the cigarettes he had in his pants pockets and burned him on his dick wit' it over and over again. He couldn't help but cry and scream more at the same time. His throat was on fire and dick was stinging from the cigarette burns. He tried to get out the chair but the ties were too tight.

"Where you goin, huh? Payback's a bitch, ain't it," said Angel.

"I'm tired of fuckin' wit' this nigga," said Symone.

She grabbed the bottle of bleach just used and poured it all over his body. She lit a piece of newspaper and threw it on him. His body went up in flames in a matter of seconds. Our work was good. We walked out the door and left him there to burn. His screams became fain't as we made our way out the building.

It was two am when Zy heard her bell ringing and somebody banging on the door. She grabbed her gun and went to peak out the window. When she peered through the blinds and saw the police cars, Zy almost shit herself. She put the gun in her safe and answered the door in a real groggy voice.

"Can I help, y'all?"

"Yes. I'm Detective O'Riley and this is my partner, Detective Samuels. Are you Zyasia Richmond?"

"Yes I am. How can I help you?"

"Ms. Richmond, we need you to come down to the station with us. We have a few questions to ask you."

"Questions about what?" Zy tried to ask tiredly so the detectives wouldn't realize just how scared she was.

"We can discuss all of that once we're at the station maam. Can you follow us there please?"

"I have a baby in the room sleep and I don't know what this about." Zy answered.

"Ok well, will you agree to come to the station first thing this morning? We have some questions for you about an alleged homicide that took place a few months ago."

"Homicide? That's murder right?" Zy asked playing dumb like she wasn't sure what it meant.

"Yes, it is. We're just following up on the incident so here's my card. Please give me a call in the morning and come on down to the station. Are we clear?"

"Yes...but...well, can I at least know who was murdered?" Zy said.

"Again, Ms. Richmond, we will discuss everything in the morning."

They turned to leave and Zy closed her door. She was nervous as hell and she knew that wasn't gonna help at all. She picked up the phone and called me.

"Hello," I answered in a sleepy voice."

"Jada, this me. Sorry to wake you up girl, but this is an emergency."

"What's wrong, Zy?" I asked concerned.

"These two fuckin' detectives just left here talking about they need me to come to the station this morning and answer some questions about an alleged murder."

"Aww shit! I'll be there in a lil while," I said and hung up.

Zy said she paced the floor back and forth for what seemed like forever. She went over and over in her head which murder they could be talking about. She was scared and all she could do was cry. She looked in on Jalen and kissed him on his forehead.

"I'm so sorry, baby. I'm so sorry. I promise if I get out of this I'm done for good with this life."

Her thoughts were interrupted by the bell ringing. It was us and for a split second she felt a sense of relief. She let us in and told us about the lil visit from the detectives.

"So let me make sure I'm hearing you right," I said. "Did he specifically use the words 'alleged murder'?"

"Yeah, that's exactly what he said."

"And, he said it happened a couple of months ago, right?"

"Yup." Zy answered.

"Ok, if he said 'allegedly' then that means they more than likely don't have a body or nuttin' so they don't know if the person was actually murdered. The only thing I think it can be is the dude we burned up and tortured. Remember, he said somethin' about telling the cops we murdered his boy?"

"Oh yeah, dats right," said Lace. "I thought dat nigga was just talkin' shit cuz he was drunk. He was a fuckin' rat fa real."

"Yeah, but if that's the case, then why did they wait so long to come around? How did they get to Zy?" Symone asked.

"Look. Right now, they just are investigating the shit. I don't think they have any evidence of any kind or they wouldn't have left and asked you to come in the morning. They would've arrested you right then and there. So they fishin' right now," I said. "When you go there tomorrow, you gotta be real careful about what you say."

"Wait. If they got to Zy then they had to talk to the chick that owns the salon," said Angel.

"You got her number right?" I asked.

"Yeah hold up. Let me get my cell," Zy said as she searched around in her oversize Gucci bag for her phone.

Zy was calling Sharon to find out if the police been by to talk to her.

"Hey, Sharon, sorry to wake you. This is Zyasia. I need to talk to you about somethin'."

"Zyasia, girl I been waiting to hear from you. Some detectives came by the shop asking me about what happened that day."

"Yeah, dats why I was callin'. They just left here," Zy said putting her on speaker.

"I told them I ain't see nuttin' that happened. They wanted to see my surveillance from the camera dat day. But, girl, I ain't stupid. I told them the tape only recorded the early part of the day and it ran out of space but I didn't know it. All it showed was the people that came in up until that point and I erased the rest."

"So how they get to me?" Zy asked curiously.

"I heard them talking about running the license plates of the cars that was in the parking lot and contacting those people to see if they saw anything. So they probably have been doing that."

"They don't have shit then," Zy stated with a sigh of relief.

"They ain't got shit from here, girl. None of us said nuttin' just like we agreed. It could've been anyone of us out there they was tryna rob so we don't blame y'all for what y'all did."

"Okay, girl, thank you and I'll be in touch," Zy responded gratefully.

She hung up the phone in relief.

"Okay, now we know they just fishin'," I said. "That dude probably did say something, but dead men can't talk. They can't get nuttin' else outta him. And, they ain't got nobody or no evidence so they can't do shit to you. When you go in the morning just say you and your friend was getting y'all hair done. When y'all came out, her car was gone and that's it. Angel made a police report sayin' the same thing so they can't do shit."

"Yeah and the clean-up crew took care of any evidence that might've been in the parking lot, blood and all, so y'all good," said Symone.

"Did y'all leave the shells out there?" I asked.

"Nah, we got em up. Girl, you taught us well." Angel said to me.

"Ok, cool. So fuck it, go there and tell 'em what I said and you good." I told her.

"Aiight. Y'all think y'all can stay here? I'ma need somebody to stay with Jalen while I go there."

"Yeah, I wanna go with you too cuz it was my car and we can tell them together that way they don't have to bother coming to knock on my door," said Angel.

"We can watch Jalen while y'all do dat," said Lace.

It was just turning four-thirty am when we took it down. Zy only had three bedrooms in her house, but we made it work for the night.

When Zy got to the police station, both detectives were there and waiting for her. They brought her in a room and asked her the same questions over and over again. She answered all of them the same way explaining to them that there was no murder that any one of them saw. Her friend's car was stolen and that was it.

"I don't know anything about a murder happening," she repeated.

Detective Samuels started getting upset after two hours of yelling and screaming saying, "We have it on tape that you killed that guy, so how long you wanna play this game, Ms. Richmond? We have all we need to make sure you and your friend out there don't see the light of day for a long time! So you might as well do ya'self a favor and tell us what the fuck happened," he screamed.

"I don't know what the fuck y'all talkin' about but you don't have me and my friend on tape doing nuttin' but going to get our hair done and leavin'. You may see us on ya fuckin' tape lookin for her car in the parkin' lot and that's it. So don't be fuckin' screamin' at me about some shit I don't know nuttin' about."

"Samuels, let me talk to Ms. Richmond alone for a second," said Detective O'Riley.

Samuels got up and left out the room slamming the door behind him.

"Look, Ms. Richmond, I know you must be scared. Those guys tried to rob you and your friend and you shot him in self-defense. If that's the case then we need to know that. We looked up the guy's history and they have a long list of charges ranging from robbery to attempted murder. So if they tried to kill y'all during that robbery then it's self-defense. But, you need to tell us that so we can move forward with this case. Right now it's first-degree murder. If it was murder in self-defense then it's a closed case. We just need to know what happened."

"Well, maybe you should tell all that to the person who killed somebody in first degree or self defense. I already told y'all I don't know what the fuck y'all talkin' about."

After another ten minutes of that, they let Zy go. When she walked out, she saw Angel just leaving out of another interrogation room as well. The detectives who questioned her looked just as frustrated as Detectives O'Riley and Samuels. They headed out the door and never looked back confident that they were in the clear.

When they got in the car they talked about all the questions they were asked and found out how each other answered.

"They tried that good cop bad cop shit wit' you too," said Zy laughing.

"Yeah, girl. I had them mad as hell in that room. They ain't got shit," Angel laughed.

ZYASIA

It wasn't gonna be easy saying goodbye to the girls or to the game. The money was plentiful and I loved them like the sisters I never had. But I made a promise to myself and to my son that if I got out of that murder thing I would give it all up.

I don't know how I'm gonna tell them but when I called Jada and asked her to get the girls together and meet me at the house, I had a feeling she knew something was up. I don't mean to hurt them though. They were there when I had nothing or no one to turn to but my mom. In the four years I've known them, they've never broken their word to me and have been there like they said they would.

I can still remember the day we met. I had just accepted what I decided would be my last collect phone call from Quan that day. He wasn't shit from the door and the only thing he ever did for me was give me my son. I will always love him for that blessing but outside of that I could care less about him for how he did us.

I had just turned twenty-three when I found out I was pregnant with Jalen. We both were so happy and Quan told his whole family how he was about to be a father. He said he was going to stop hustling and leave the street life alone, soon as he stacked a lil bit of money for us to be good with.

That proved to be all lies and broken promises as usual. He still stayed out all night and came home when he felt like it. He couldn't have been out hustling all night cuz his ass never had no money when he got home. Not no real money anyways. I mean, he gave me money to buy food and pay the rent, always late, but that was about it.

I found out a bit too late that the real reason I never saw my man was because the muthafucka wasn't *my* man. I remember the naïve shit I use to go for like it was yesterday. Like the day Quan came home smelling real different. I knew the smell wasn't a perfume or scented lotion that I owned. Nah, the shit smelled too expensive for my pockets.

So once again, we fought. I hit him with everything I could find in sight. After he finally calmed me down, he swore that the smell had to be his mothers' perfume. He told me how he was over there and she kept holding him, begging him to leave those streets alone because of some dream she had. He swore that's all it was. So after all the screaming, yelling and accusing him I did I felt like shit. I believed him so to make it up, I fucked my man like my life depended on making him feel like no other.

A few days later came the call that no chick ever wants to get. The chick on the other end introduced herself as Tamyra, Quan's wifey. She told me how they have been together for five years and she was tired of playing this game. She said she always knew about me but it didn't matter to her. I was just something Quan did when she didn't feel like putting up with his shit. She said I been running around claiming to be his wifey but she felt like she needed to end the bullshit. I was the mistress, not the wife.

She told me that she and Quan were going to get married so I need to leave him alone. She told me how she knew he paid my rent and that all was about to stop. She was not going stop him from taking care of the baby but that was it. The fucking and sucking on her man was done.

I wanted to kill this nigga. He had me running around for two years like I was the one. Had me thinking we were about to be a family and shit when he knew he had a wifey all this time. I was the side chick and if it wasn't for the life that was growing in my belly I probably would've done some weak ass shit like killed myself. That's how dumb I was over this nigga.

Sometimes when I think about it, it's like I can still taste the tears that streamed into my mouth. I was beyond hurt. After I bleached his clothes and broke up everything else of his I could find, I sat and waited for him to get home. When I heard the keys I jumped up and opened the door before he had a chance to turn the key good. I hit him with everything I could grab before he finally pinned me down. I remember screaming at him that I know about Tamyra and me and him were done. I told him I was going to keep my baby and I didn't need him to do shit for us. I guess he understood the place I was at. He didn't even try to explain, he knew it was no way to ease that type of hurt. Instead, he wiped my tears, gave me a wad of money, and walked out the door.

He came by a few times after I had Jalen. He would sit and play with him for a minute then try to get me to fuck him. When he saw he wasn't getting any ass from me, he would throw a few hundred dollars on the table and leave. It was the same thing every time he came by until he just stopped coming. A few months after that is when I got the first collect call from him and found out he was locked up. He took a plea deal and got ten years for his part in helping to rob a check-cashing place.

I took his calls every now and then but I wasn't too beat for him. He ruined me as far as I was concerned. He would ask me to bring the baby to see him and when I refused it always turned into an argument. I would tell him I wasn't bringing my baby to a filthy ass jail and when he was on the streets he didn't give a damn about seeing him, so it wasn't happening. That last time we spoke, I told him I needed to go get Jalen some pampers and I was tired of arguing with him. I told him not call my house no more and hung up. I haven't accepted a call from him since.

I went to the grocery store hoping that the new counterfeit money I made was better than before so I could get the baby what he needed. But the bitch on the register pulled my card and caused a big ass scene about it. I walked out of there mad as hell and my baby still didn't have what he needed. I didn't get paid for another three days so I knew I would have to call my mother and get some money from her as usual.

Then I met Jada and Lace and the rest is history. But when I started out I was only trying to get some money to get right with. I didn't know that it would get this deep between all of us or in the game. Last month when those detectives came at me, I just knew my lil black ass was done. But now I think it's time I make good on my promise to myself and my baby before I'm not so lucky next time. I'm sitting tight on eight point six million now so me and my baby about to get the hell out of P.A. I tried to talk the girls into getting out but they not trying to hear it. So I gotta do me.

When I got to the house to meet with everybody I was nervous as hell. I didn't know what to expect. I mean, I know I loved these girls and they loved me but this shit was like the mafia right now. Who knows if they gotta problem with you try'na get out of the game.

I had a whole speech planned out in my head before I got there. I knew exactly what I was gonna say. But when I opened my mouth nothing that I had ready would come out so I just spoke the truth from my heart.

"Y'all know that I been talkin' about us getting out the game lately. I know y'all not feelin' me on that so I'm not gon try to convince y'all otherwise. We all grown and have to make our own decisions and I respect dat you know. But it's time for me to let this go. When I met y'all I was fucked up in the game and y'all helped to give me and my son a new life," I said through teary eyes.

"Y'all know that I appreciate everything y'all do for me and I would never turn my back on y'all, so I hope that's not how y'all look at it. I have to do this for me and my baby while I can. Everyday, I think about what could happen' wit' me being out here in these streets like this. How many more people I'ma have to kill, or will I get locked up one day, or will one of these hatin' ass mutha fuckas kill me? I think about all of that. The bottom line is what's gon' happen to my baby? I been wanting to stop for a while now, but I didn't want to leave knowing y'all needed me when we got the coke. I feel like y'all good now and as hard as it is, I have to go. I hope that we still a team and y'all still my sisters. Just because I ain't running wit' y'all no more, don't mean we still not a family. So I hope y'all good with my decision."

The living room was so quiet you could hear people breathing. They all looked at me with a blank look on their faces and I couldn't read what they were thinking for the first time in a long time. They got up one by one and walked out the room. I sat up on the couch with my hands open as if to say, 'Where y'all goin?'

"How y'all just gon' get up and leave like dat? Y'all don't have nuttin' to say?"

I sat in the living room for about five minutes crying before I stood up to leave. When I walked towards the door everybody ran to me singing, "*We just playin' girrrl*". They hugged me and told me to come back in the livin' room.

"We got a surprise for you," Jada said.

"We been knew you wanted to be out, ma, we was just waitin' for you to come tell us, ya feel me?" Said Lace while sitting next to me with her arm around my shoulders.

Jada handed me the manila folder and told me to open it.

"What the hell y'all, bitches up to now?" I said.

I opened the folder to find what looked liked printouts and layouts for a mansion.

"I don't get it. What's this?" I asked with a confused look at my girls.

"That's ya new house in Atlanta," said Angel.

"What!! You bullshittin', right?"

"Nope," Jada continued. "Like Lace said, we knew you were ready to leave a year ago. Symone told me how you be online lookin' at houses in Atlanta. So last year we all chipped in to have you, Jalen and your mom a new house built out there. Look at this shit," said Jada sittin down next to her.

Everybody crowded around to look at the pictures of the house with me.

"I can't believe y'all did this. This ain't no fuckin house! It's a mansion! This shit had to cost millions. Look at this," I said going through the pages, "seven bedrooms and five bathrooms. Daaaamn! And it has a guesthouse too!! Look at the pool oh my God! This is so beautiful. Thank y'all sooooo much," I cried huggin' all of them.

"You welcome, girl. It's almost done. The builders said it'll be ready in two more months. So you and Jalen and ya mom get ready, girl," said Symone.

"Oh shit…my mother! I gotta go tell her!" I shouted happily.

"Girl, ya mother been knew. She helped wit' it all," said Lace laughing.

"And her house is already sold," said Angel.

"How the fuck did y'all pull this off wit'' out me knowing?"

"The same way we make millions wit' out the Feds knowing," said Lace sarcastically.

JADA

We were finally down to our last fifty keys and we knew that shit would be gone in less than two weeks. I needed to get in touch with the dude in Cuba and set up a shipment like yesterday. I called the number that Rubin had given me not knowing what to expect. A man with a heavy accent answered the phone.

"Can I speak to Armando?" I asked.

"Who wants to know?"

"Dis Jada, from P.A.. Rubin said I could call you."

"Oh yes! The very beautiful Jada I heard so much about."

"Yeah, beautiful and low on product."

"You cannot be done already. Was that a lot of powder to get rid of?" He said, more in a way of asking a question than making a statement.

I giggled to myself thinking, *These muthafucka's and their accents are funny as hell.*

"Yeah, well, I'm pretty much done so can I get some more or what?"

"Ok, mami. I know you don't want as much as you had before. That's too expensive."

"How much is half dat amount?" I asked.

"Look, mami, I'll tell you what, since you're a friend of Rubin's, I will send you whatever you need. You pay me half now, half later. Sound good?"

"Yeah that'll work. So how do I get it here?"

"Well, that depends. You can have it flown in or brought in on the water."

"How much?" I asked.

"Again, because your Rubin's friend, either one I will have done for two hundred thousand dollars." He told me like it was a deal.

"Alright well, by air seems like the fastest, so I'll take that." I told him.

"Ok, I will have it ready in one week for you. You will need a truck. Maybe, a moving truck when it comes?"

"Yeah I know," I answered him. "So, I'll call you in a week then. Thanks, Armando."

I walked across the hall to Laces' room to let her know I ordered some more work. When I opened the door and didn't see her, I went downstairs to Symone's room. I could hear her on the phone arguing with somebody. I stood on the stairwell leaned up against the wall and listened for a minute before I went down. The shit sounded a lil funny to me but I didn't wanna draw up no conclusions.

"Don't you think I know dat?" Symone asked. "I can't take it from what we got now, I gotta wait for the re-up then I'ma hit y'all off." Symone's voice got louder and she sounded real annoyed with whoever was on the other end of that phone.

"Man, they don't know shit. They don't check it like they should to realize when a few keys are missin'. You all paranoid for nuttin'." I heard silence for a minute. Then Symone continued. "I know we losin' money but I told you I can't do nuttin' 'bout dat right now. When I can, I'll holla."

I heard the sound the cell makes when you hit the end button. I knew Symone must've hung up the phone. I crept back upstairs as quietly as I could. I could hear noises coming from the kitchen and hoped it was Lace. I was furious and wasn't sure how I was going to handle the shit.

Maybe I heard her wrong, I thought to myself. No matter how much I tried to reason with myself, it wasn't working. I heard what I heard and the shit sounded shady as hell. I just know Symone is on some snake-shit.

I found Lace in the kitchen making a turkey and cheese sandwich.

"Wass' up chica? You hungry? I can hook you up!"

"Nah I'm good but come up stairs for a minute with me." I told her.

"You aiight? Why you look so mad?" Lace asked me in a concerned voice.

"Yo! I just heard some shit and before I kill this bitch in here you need to come upstairs wit' me right quick."

Lace left the food on the counter and followed me. We went in my room and I told her about the conversation I just over-heard Symone having with an unidentified caller.

"That can't be what you heard, ma." Lace replied after I told her what I had over-heard.

"I know what the fuck I heard Lace, and I'm tellin' you that's what she said on the phone! Last week she wanted to put the order in for the work herself but I told her Rubin made it clear that the guy would only deal wit' me on dat and she was actin' kinda funny then but I ain't think nuttin of it. Now dis shit."

"Yo, on some real shit, you know how I feel about snake ass bitches. I'ma handle dis shit right now," said Lace, grabbing her .22 from on top of her closet.

"No! I wanna see what she up to. The new work gon' be here in a week so have Angel reserve a U-Haul. If this bitch been stealin' from us, it's over!" I told her.

"Man why we gotta wait for all lat? Let me handle da bitch right now and be done wit' it." Lace begged. She was ready to put Symone to sleep, right this second.

"Cuz she suppose to be our girl, dat's why. It's bad enough we gotta kill her ass if she on some other shit, but at least find out what she up to."

"All I need to know is the bitch tryna play us and dats enough for me to do what I gotta do. But I'll wait like you said." Lace said.

A week later, the new work got there. Nothing seemed out of the ordinary with Symone. She didn't fuck up the count like we thought she would try to do. None of the money was short for her orders or anything like that. Lace and I felt bad for thinking she was being shiesty.

A few weeks later, Angel sat and repeatedly counted the keys. I had her keeping track of everything since that Symone thing happened. Each time she got the same result. They were five keys short. Angel solemnly walked into my bedroom to let me know the count was off.

"Jada, I just did the count and we five keys short."

"You sure there wasn't any orders you missed?" I asked her, not wanting to believe it.

"Nah I doubled checked everything. The count was right three days ago. No new orders came in yet. But we still five keys short." Angel said again.

"Wait a few days and see if money comes in for them ok. And whatever you do, don't let Lace know nuttin missin' yet. I think I know what happened to 'em but I want to be sure."

"Aiight."

I was furious. I knew Lace would kill Symone as soon as she found out so I kept the news to myself.

Just when I thought I was wrong about the chick she played me, I hope for her sake she turn up wit' the money for those keys or she gon' die a slow and painful death for crossin' us.

SYMONE

S ymone dropped off the five keys to her brother so him and his boy could sell it. She had been taking a few keys here and there so her brother could make some money. She wanted to make a lil something on the side for herself too.

Jada wanna run shit like we all work for her or sumthin. Fuck dat! Symone don't work for no fuckin' body! I set up my own shit to run on the side and I'm the head bitch in charge over here. I asked her to let me holla at the connect and I could've done it the right way but she wanna run the show and don't want us to be able to get the coke wit' out her. If that's how she wanna do it then that's how we gon' do it then. I'm just gon' continue to take what I need. All money gotta be split five ways. Well, four now that Zy scary ass left. But either way, that's whack. I'm tryna make dis money so I can be out too.

Symone's thoughts ran crazy as she drove to her brothers stash house. When she got there him and his boy was in there playing the X-Box 360 game yelling about who was getting they ass whopped in the boxing match.

"Turn that shit off," Symone said. She loved the feeling of being in control. She didn't give a damn if it was her brother or not. She was running the show and she liked it.

"Yo, it's about time. I swear you be on some bull hit. These niggas out here getting money while I'm losing money," Symone's brother greedily told her.

"Yeah, well you can shut shit down out here wit' dis," Symone said putting the five keys on the table in the kitchen.

"Dats Wass' up. But on the real, big sis, I don't see why you don't let me and my niggas run down on them chicks you run wit'.

You know my soldiers trained to kill so we can take it over for real and you ain't even gotta do it like dis no more."

"Hell nah. This is still my bread and butter nigga. This lil shit we doin' ain't shit compared to what me and the girls do. This just help me get a lil more dats it."

"Dats what I'm sayin'. We ain't doin' shit right now like how we could be doin' it if we had it all."

Y'all niggas run down if y'all want to on them and y'all liable to get y'all whole fuckin' heads blown off. They not to be fucked wit' and I keep tellin' y'all dat."

"You scared of dem? I know you can't be scared of dem! What you think they gon' do if they find out what you been doin'? You might as well let me take care of that now so you ain't even gotta worry 'bout it."

"Nigga, I ain't scared of shit. You better know dat. But I ain't stupid either. I get money wit' these chicks and I ain't about to fuck dat up cuz you and ya boys wanna take over. Plus Jada the only one wit' the connect."

"When we done with her fine ass, she gon' give up the connect. Trust me. I been wantin' to fuck her for a minute now," he laughed giving his boy a pound.

"Nigga, you wish she would let you pipe. She would dis ya ass in ya dreams," laughed Symone.

"She ain't gotta let me. I'll take the pussy then let my lil niggas scrape those walls. When we get done, we gon know it all."

"I'm out. Y'all done lost y'all damn minds. Stick to the program and y'all gon eat aiight?"

"Aiight! Fuck it we can chill for a minute. We gettin' these keys for free, so we good for now."

"Ain't shit free, nigga! Y'all better have my paper or its gon' be a problem." Symone told them.

"You know we got dis! Chill, sis!"

SYMONE

Symone drove home thinking about what it would be like to be on top 'wit' out' the other girls. If she had this whole shipment to herself then she wouldn't need them any more. She could get out too with this shipment alone. It was worth millions and she wouldn't worry about the 'connect' or needing to get more. She would be done with the drug game. The sirens behind her interrupted her thoughts. She looked in her rear view mirror to see an unmarked police car behind her. *Damn,* she thought as she pulled over to the shoulder of the road. *I must've been speeding.* She watched as the two officers, one male and one female, got out and approached her car.

"Maam, can I see your license and registration please?" The female officer asked.

"What did I do?" Symone asked as she reached in the glove box for her registration.

"You were observed going into and leaving out of a well known drug house. Please step out of the vehicle."

"I don't know nuttin' about no drug house," Symone said while exiting the car.

"Do you mind if we search your vehicle, maam?" asked the male cop. He was in a cheap suit so Symone knew he had to be a detective.

"Do y'all have a warrant to search my car?"

"No we don't," the detective replied.

"Then y'all not searchin' my car."

"We do have a right to search the vehicle, maam, if we believe there are drugs or weapons in the car. Also you were seen entering the house with a duffel bag that looked full at the time. When you came out it was clear there was nothing in it. So based on that, you have now become a part of our investigation," the female officer said as she searched her. "Do you have anything in your pockets that could cut or poke me?"

"Do you see pockets on anything I have on?" Symone replied.

"Please take a seat back here," said the female officer placing Symone in the back seat of the car.

She watched as they searched her car trying their hardest to find something. She saw the male officer grab the black duffel she was carrying and look through it. He smelled it, looking for any indication there was drugs in it at some point. When they didn't find anything she could see the look of frustration on their faces.

"What was in the bag?" The male officer asked.

"My brother's clothes. He left them at my house, so I dropped them off to him."

The cops got back in the car and turned to face Symone.

"Listen," started the male detective. "We know there was a lot more than clothes in that bag. We been watching you come and go from that house for quite some time now. All we need to know is who the supplier is. We don't want you, your brother or the little dealers. We want the supplier. Now, we do know that you supply your brother and his team. That's obvious by the way there's very little movement in the streets until you come around with your little duffel bags."

"So, where do you get it?" the female officer asked. "That's who we want. You tell us who it is and testify in court and you walk. Or you go down for a real long time with your brother and the rest of 'em."

"I don't supply nuttin' to nobody. I didn't know it was a crime for me to visit my brother."

"Don't play games with us. We know a lot more than you think we know. You have two weeks to get us that information or you and your brother are done. And don't think about leaving, I assure you, you won't get far."

They let Symone out the car and handed her a card with their information on it. Symone walked back to her car with a numb look on her face.

How the hell did I get myself into this? She thought. She pulled off with the cops watching her. *I know I shouldn't have started this. Jada always said messin' wit' the nickel and dime money was a sure way to get caught. She always warned us not to do business in that area. I broke all the rules try'na get money on the side. Now what I'ma do? I betrayed them to have to deal with dis shit now alone. I guess this what they mean about Karma.*

JADA

A week had gone by since Angel told me about the missing keys. I knew I had to tell Lace what was going on. Symone been trying harder and harder to get me to give up the connect and now I knew why. She wanted to do her own thing. But if that was the case then she could've just said something. Going against us wasn't necessary. I followed her when she left the house the other day and saw her go to her brother's house. I had a feeling that's where the missing keys went. I knew it was time to do what I had to do. They say keep your enemies close and your friends closer. I know why now.

SYMONE

I was on edge. Those detectives been hounding me for the connect info and who was our supplier. I had to give them something. I knew Jada wasn't going to budge on telling me who he was. I tried everything. I made it seem like one of our biggest customers wanted to do business with him so he could supply the west coast. I even told Jada the guy said he would bring us in if we wanted. Jada still wasn't hearin' it. She said if that's what he wanted, then we could supply him.

"That's crazy paper for us," Jada said. "We don't need it. We good on our end."

Dis bitch just don't get it, I thought. *All she thinks about is herself. She probably wouldn't give a damn if she knew that they were gon' run down on me and my brother. If it weren't for us setting up our earlier businesses with the real estate scam and making sure we had fake identification, half the shit we did wouldn't have gotten done like it did. Now she don't trust me?*

With only two days left to get the connect, I knew I had to make that call. There was no way I would be able to get the connect. I refused to go to jail because Jada wanted to be in control of it all. I just can't.

M̲e, Lace and Angel went to one of our favorite restaurants for dinner so we could talk. I didn't want to talk
about it in the house, and I had a taste for lobster tails so
we went to "Outback Steakhouse". We waited until the waiter finished taking our orders before we started talking. We all ordered
the same thing. Three lobster tails steamed. A loaded baked potato
and a house salad. When the waiter left I started.

I told Angel about the call I overheard a few weeks ago and
me and Lace decided to handle it. Then I told Lace what Angel
told me about the missing keys and how I handled that too. Once
everybody was brought up to speed we had to figure what we
wanted to do about Symone.

"Man, I told you, you should a let me kill the bitch in the first
place," said Lace. "She crossed us and it ain't no telling what else
the bitch up too!"

Lace was furious, all she wanted was to go home and wait for
Symone to get there.

"I had no idea she was on it like dat. But now that I think
about it, we were short a few times before. I just thought I had
miscounted or something," said Angel.

"Nah, you wasn't miscounting, ma. That shady bitch was robbing us so her and her brother can do them. But it's all good. She
got it coming. I'ma cut that bitch fingers off one by one since she
wanna be a thief. Then I'ma cut her fuckin tongue out her mouth
for all the lies she been running around telling. One thing is for
sure, we're gonna make that bitch open her safe and take all that
dough out before we kill her ass," I told them.

119

"Oh, most definitely!" Said Angel. "And I'ma burn that stash house down with them niggas in it. Guaranteed!"

We sat back and ate our dinner without another word about Symone.

By the time we finished eating dinner, our phones were going crazy. All three of them were ringing back to back. Some calls were from Symone's cell, others from her brothers and others from numbers we didn't recognize.

We paid the bill and left thinking it had to be an emergency. I called Symone's cell first. I was surprised when a man answered instead of her.

"Who's this?" I asked.

"This is Detective Rogers with homicide. Is this Jada?"

Aww, damn here we go again. I thought.

"Yes. This is Jada."

"Jada, I'm afraid I have some bad news for you. It seems that a friend of yours has been murdered. We needed to know if you have away to reach her next of kin."

"What friend?" I asked incredulously.

"Symone Mitchell and her brother Shawn Mitchell were killed earlier today. It looks like it was a drug deal gone bad. I'm sorry to have to tell you this. Do you know how to reach their next of kin?"

"You just did. They don't have any other family," I said smugly.

Lace and Angel was on edge waiting for me to tell them what was going on.

"Ok...well, we need someone to come down and identify the bodies. I'm sure you want to have a memorial service for them as well."

"No I can't stand to see them that way. If you say it's her then it's her."

"Well, it's procedure, maam. Can you at least identify any tattoos on the deceased as a confirmation?"

"Yeah, she has tattoo of a butterfly on her right wrist and puppy paws on her thigh." I told the detective, describing Symone's tattoos.

"Ok, that will be fine. Again I'm sorry for your loss. Will you be making arrangements to pick up the body?"

"No the State can do what they want. Thanks for calling," I said and hung up.

"What the hell happened?" said Lace.

I told them what the detective said and they looked like they were in shock.

"Damn! That's some fucked up shit. But Karma is a mutha-fucka," said Lace. "They lucky they got to her before we did."

"I don't even know how to digest all this shit right now," said Angel. "I need a fuckin' drink."

I turned the key in the truck and pulled out of the parking lot.

"There ain't nothing to digest, she had it coming," said Lace.

"Angel, call the place that installed our safes tomorrow and have them come open her shit," I said. "Lace you can help me pack all her shit up. I'm donating it to the Salvation Army."

JADA

It's been a year since Symone was killed and longer since Zy left but we still was on the grind. Symone had cleared her safe of all the money. We found that out when we had the company come open it, so we knew that she was up to no good. Her disloyalty didn't stop us though. We decided to expand our client base to include parts of the south. We still weren't ready for the west coast just yet but we damn sure were working on it.

We found it easier to divide states between the three of us after we added the Carolinas, Georgia and Florida to our supply chain. It made shit flow a lil better knowing exactly who handled what. The money was coming non-stop and we found ourselves running out of coke faster and faster with each shipment. It became obvious that we needed to double our re-up amount.

Of course, Armando ain't have no problem wit' it. We were making his ass a killing. He told me that he never heard of females selling the amount of powder we did and so fast. I keep telling these niggas out here we far from the average females but they don't seem to be hearing me. We didn't waste time chasing dick or club hopping every night. As far as we was concerned, there wasn't a nigga out there that could take care of us better than we could ourselves so what was the point?

We got fucked when we needed too and nothing more. A nigga would be lucky if he got a number to call us afterwards. Shit, the way I see it, niggas been doing this shit forever. Why can't a chick be all about her paper too?

With my schedule in full swing all day, I felt I needed a warm shower. My thoughts went into overdrive as I let the steam calm me. I just wanted ten minutes without having to think about anything. But when I heard the knock on the bathroom door, I knew I wouldn't get it. I wiped the fog off the glass shower door just enough to see through it.

"Jada!"

"Come in." She did. "Wass' up, Angel?"

"You think you can come wit' me today to make dis drop? It's a new customer and he wants four keys. But for some reason I don't trust this clown. His whole swagger seem to fake, you know?"

"Where he from?"

"He is comin' from South Carolina." Angel replied.

I rinsed the last of the soap off my body and turned off the shower. I slid the glass door open and reached for my bathrobe that was hanging up. Angel watched as I wrapped my hair in a towel before responding.

"Yeah, I can come with you. Where are you meeting them at?"

"At the Grey Hound bus station, in an hour."

"Ok, let me get ready and we can go." I told my friend.

When Angel and I got to the station, we watched as people got off the bus. When Angel spotted him she got out and watched as he sat on the bench.

She was sure he said it would be two of them but she didn't see anyone else. She went and sat on the bench next to him like she didn't know him.

"Wass' up, Will?" She said looking away from him. "Is it all here?"

"Yeah, it's all here. You got my shit?"

"I need to count this. You can chill for a while and I'll call you and tell you where to get it from."

"You expect me to let you walk off wit' my bread and wait for you to call me? Hell nah, I'm comin' wit' you, shorty."

"You're not going anywhere wit' me, dude. Dis how I work. If you ain't feelin' it I can leave ya bag right here. I'm many things but a thief ain't never been one of 'em. So, choose quickly. Don't waste my time."

"If I don't hear from you in an hour, I swear I will find you and murder ya whole family, shorty."

"Don't threaten me, muthafucka. Y'all some paranoid ass niggas, but wanna be bosses," she said as she picked up the bag and walked off.

I started the car when I saw Angel coming. We pulled off and went to the motel to count the money. It took a lil longer than we expected but she called the dude every twenty minutes to let him know she was good. When we were done, we realized the money was short by two hundred thousand dollars. Angel got on the phone and called the dude again.

"You short, B."

"Bitch, ain't nuttin short!" He shouted into the phone.

"Nigga, its short by two hundred, so you gone be a few pounds lighter."

"I want what I said and nuttin' less! My guy and I counted the shit twice and it was correct."

"Well either you missed counted it or ya boy got you. Either way the shit short. I ain't in the business of arguing, so what you wanna do?"

I looked out the window just in time to see the guy who was supposed to be waiting at the Greyhound station, getting out a car with another dude. He was still talking on the cell with Angel. I could tell it was a set up. I whispered to Angel and told her to look out the window. She hung up the phone while he was still talking realizing he was stalling for time.

We threw all the money back in the bag and left it there. Before the guys could get in the door good, we ran out the room and hid in the hallway leading to the next floor up. When we saw them turn the corner down the hall heading in the wrong direction, we dashed out the emergency door and ran for the car.

I hit the auto start on my key chain and unlocked the doors as we ran towards the truck. We hopped in and I peeled off causing a screeching sound with my tires. When we were out of harm's way, Angel called the dude back.

"Room one-zero-three, you thirsty, muthafucka." Angel told him.

"Yeah, I see y'all bitches got the hell out of dodge, huh! Stupid, bitch, you ain't even take the money!"

"I told you already you starvin', bastard, I ain't neva been a thief. You can keep ya change. That's shoe money for me. And to show you it ain't no hard feelings about you and ya broke ass boy tryna set us up, we left y'all a lil sumthin in the bathroom cabinet."

I set the jug of acid to fall down as soon as the cabinet door was opened. I knew if it came down to it, those niggas would get suspicious enough to open it. When Angel told me she didn't trust the dude, I wasn't gonna take any chances. Your first instinct is usually the right one. We stopped off at the room and she set it up just in case before going to the bus station.

That night, me, Angel and Lace were chillin in the living room watching the news and eating. When we heard the hotels name, we all looked up and got real quiet. Lace turned the volume up so we could hear it better.

The reporter was saying how the ambulance responded to a call where two men were found burned from the top of their head down to their backs. He said acid burns caused the injuries. They said the men were not the ones who rented the room and the hotel manager had no idea what they were doing there.

The men were unable to speak due to the injuries sustained the reporter continued but it seems that they were trying to say something about their money. The hotel manager reported that he responded to a complaint from other guests of loud screaming coming from the room but there was no money in there so he didn't know what the guys could be talking about.

We all laughed when the segment ended.

"Aaahh!! Who the dumb ones now?" Angel said at the TV screen.

"You know that manager got that dough," I laughed.

"Y'all crazy as hell for dat shit right there," Lace chuckled.

"These niggas gon' learn one day that we can't be touched," I said with confidence.

"Speaking of that, Ms. Untouchable," said Lace, "don't you think it's time for us to get the powder out this house?"

"Yeah, I was thinking about that too. I don't trust stash houses though, but I know we need one."

"We can rent a lil one bed room somewhere and I'll make it as secure as possible. Put some cameras up and the best locks on the doors. And I'll have some more safes installed over there too," said Lace. "But we can't keep this here too much longer know what I mean?"

"You right," I said. "Well, do what you do then, when you ready, we'll move it."

"Aiight, I'm on top of it."

JADA

I was in a panic trying to reach Lace and Angel. I knew they were home but they weren't answering their phones. It was two o'clock in the morning, so I was sure they had to be sleep. I had just left from visiting Rubin and what he told me had me going crazy. Rubin was right when he said he knew information nobody else knew.

He had been schooling me about lil things I should and shouldn't do in the game. But when he called me and told me I needed to come see him right away I had no idea what he was about to tell me.

He said he had a snitch on payroll with the police department and it was brought to his attention that they have been under investigation for two years. He had the guy killed for not telling him sooner all the details of the investigation. But what he did know is that they were coming at six in the morning.

"They are trying to get the warrant signed by the judge as we speak Jada. You must move everything you have to a different location. I have some help for you outside. Those guys will move anything you need."

Those words echoed in my head as I rushed to get home.

When I got there, I ran up the stairs and woke the girls up.

"Lace! Angel! Get up!" I yelled.

They both came running out of their rooms with a confused look on their faces.

"We gotta get the money out of here and move everything from the stash house too! The Feds gon run down at six o'clock. I don't have time to explain it, but we gotta move this stuff."

They ran downstairs to clean out the safes first. They put their money in garbage bags and brought it out to my truck like I had told them to do.

"I have the perfect place to hide the money don't worry." I told them.

They went back in and Angel cleared all the file cabinets. They held all the information from when we first started with the realty scams all the way up to the present.

"Throw all that shit in the fireplace. We should've never kept all those records here anyway," I said.

Lace was busy disconnecting the computers in the house. There was no time to try to clear files from the hard drive so she took all three of them out. She had the guys Rubin sent that were waiting outside come in and carry them out to the truck they had.

"We gotta get to the stash house!" I said. "Y'all done in here?"

"Yeah I'm good." Lace answered.

"Me too." Angel yelled.

We all got in our cars and the truck followed us to the stash house. The guys carried out the boxes and loaded them onto the truck. We all cleared the file cabinet there too. When we were done, we cleaned the house with all types of cleaners so the smell of coke could not be picked up. By then it was four thirty in the morning. The guys took the truck and everything in it to wherever Rubin told them to take it. I trusted him with my life, so I was sure it was fine.

"Ok, I want y'all to clean y'all cars out real good and go back home. I'll be there in a lil while. I'm going to put our money up."

"Where you takin' it?" asked Lace.

"Somewhere they will never find it!" I replied.

By the time I got back to the house the Fed's were already there. There were police cars everywhere. They even had the SWAT truck out there.

What the fuck did they think we was gon' do? I thought. *Kill a few cops and risk going to jail for the rest of our lives?*

They had Lace and Angel handcuffed and sitting in the back of a police car. I pulled in and got out like I had no idea what was going on. They immediately cuffed me and showed me the search warrant. They put me in the same car as Angel and she was glad.

"I ain't gon' lie, Jada, we thought you weren't comin' back for a minute," Angel whispered.

"I would never do y'all like dat. But I understand why you would think that way. Fear is a muthafucka. But y'all my sisters."

"It never crossed ya mind to just leave? Not even once?" Angel teased. "You had all the money and everything else too."

"Honestly?"

"Yeah. Keep it real," Angel said.

"Not once did it enter my mind to leave y'all hangin like dat." I told her sincerely.

"Dats Wass' up."

"Y'all didn't say nuttin to them right, when they ran down?" I asked.

"Nah, we know better. They bashed the door in and we were in the kitchen eating," laughed Angel. "We made ourselves known and got on the floor. They showed us the warrant and kept asking where you were at after they read us our rights. We just said we wanted our lawyer and we weren't saying shit."

"Good. Fuck these pigs," I laughed. "I don't trust these cars either so let's be quiet. These shits are bugged sometimes. That's probably why they put us in the same car. To see if we say some incriminating shit."

"CSI, huh?" Angel laughed.

"You know it." I laughed back.

When we got to the police station they laid it all out for us. We had a nine-page indictment and were being charged with everything from fraud and conspiracy to committing fraud from the realty scams, credit cards, and counterfeit money to the drugs

We all the new drill and knew not to tell them a damn thing no matter what they said. We knew once we said we wanted our lawyer, they couldn't do nothing but book us. Rubin already set us up with a lawyer. He said it would be best if we all used the same lawyer and he had the best firm in the business for us. They were known for winning cases everyone said couldn't be won.

My lawyer, Edward Pacatino, was what I could only describe as dapper as hell. He was what some called the Donald Trump of law. He was known for his sexy swagger in the courtroom and dominating tone of voice he used on cross-examinations. I was told he was very sarcastic almost to the point of being an ass-hole and if you didn't know any better you would assume he was with the mob and not a lawyer.

That's exactly what I needed in my corner, a beast in every sense of the word in that courtroom. It didn't hurt that he was fine as hell too and dressed in Armani suits that were tailored to perfection to fit his six-two, two hundred pound solid frame.

When he first met with us, he told me there was no bail but he had to wait for the arraignment to see what happened. He said he would immediately file for that to be overturned. He already knew all about what we were in to so he let me know that I had to be honest with him about everything. If I left any stone unturned, it could cost us the trial. He advised me that he didn't give a damn if I was guilty or not, it was his job to prove that I wasn't and that's the bottom line.

I told him everything from the beginning exactly how it went down, up until the time they ran down on us. He was extremely concerned with the murders.

"And you're sure they don't have any of the bodies?"

"I'm almost positive," I said.

"What's almost?" he asked concerned.

"Well, we never knew where they were taking the bodies. Once they did their thing, it was done. None of them ever turned up as far as we knew."

"Who were the guys?" Pacatino asked me.

"We never knew. A different girl took care of that but she is dead now."

"Did y'all kill her too?"

"No. Her and her brother was killed in a bad drug deal. We had nuttin' to do wit' it."

He continued to take notes as we talked for hours. I gave all the details of the realty scam and how we ran the credit cards. We all agreed that we would never mention Zy no matter what happened, being that she was out. So when I told him about the counterfeit money I left her out. I made it seem like it was us and I was sure Lace and Angel did the same. We made a pact about that.

When he left, I wondered if me not mentioning Zy would play a major part like he said.

No stones unturned, rang in my head as I lay on the lifeless cold mattress in the cell. It didn't matter. My word is my bond so if it cost me, then it cost me. I wasn't saying anything about Zy, no matter what.

"Thanks for joining us. I'm Lori Chandler. Today on *The Best Defense* on Tru T.V., nearly eight months after the indictment of the Pennsylvania Queen Pins as they have been called, the trial finally begins. The trial was initially scheduled to begin two days ago but didn't due to the defense's controversial arguments of the prosecution withholding information as to the identity of their key witness.

"The date was pushed back. The prosecution argued that it was extremely crucial that the witnesses' identity only be released to the judge and jury for their protection. They argued that the defendants were very powerful and dangerous and the witness was in fear for her life. This turned into a heated argument between the counselors with the defense arguing that the prosecution is making false statements in the presence of the jury, which could impact their initial perception of the defendants before hearing any facts about the case.

"Pacatino also argued that without the defense team knowing all witnesses expected to testify, especially the key witness, it cripples the defense from properly preparing their defense and it could cost his clients their freedom.

"Both sides had very valid arguments but in the end the judge excused the jury from the courtroom advising them to strike everything that they've heard thus far. He eventually ruled in favor of the Defense and stated that based on the VI amendment, the defendants had a right to face their accusers in a court of law. Tru T V's Michael Hensley was in the court room today and here's a look at the opening statements."

State: *"Good morning ladies and gentleman of the jury. I'm Assistant State's Attorney, Anthony Kilmer. During this trial you* will hear very emotional testimony from the people that have been affected by the actions of the defendants. We intend to prove to you that these three women did in fact fraudulently claim to be representatives of a realty company and take hundreds of thousands of dollars from innocent and unsuspecting renters.

"We will show that the defendants did willfully and intentionally use their place of employment at the time to obtain credit information from customers to use in their scam of duplicating credit cards to purchase various items for their personal use.

"You will hear how they sold millions of dollars worth of cocaine to people not only in the state of Pennsylvania but more than a half dozen other states as well. You'll hear how they counterfeited our governments' money to gain millions.

"Furthermore you will hear heartbreaking testimony from the friends and family of some of the victims of these murders. You will hear the defense argue that there were no murders. But the testimony of one witness will prove that these disappearances were not just random and coincidental. They were in fact murders, cleverly covered up to hide all evidence.

"It was a ruthless obliteration of these young lives. You'll see that once you hear the shocking testimony of the gruesome way they were killed and the cold and heartless manner in which their bodies were disposed of. The state will prove that the parties responsible for these acts are none other than the defendants, Jada Cruz, Solace Ford and Angel Washington. Thank you for your attention."

Lace, Angel and I sat back listening to what the guy was saying about us. We wondered what our lawyer had prepared to say in his opening statement. We were nervous already and it showed all over our faces.

Edward Pacatino consulted briefly with his team while rummaging through a folder before he finally stood up. When he spoke, his presence was immediately felt throughout the courtroom.

Defense: "Ladies and gentleman of the jury. Good morning to you all. My name's Attorney Edward Pacatino on behalf of the defense. Let me just start by saying that you've already heard the *outlandish statements made by the prosecution about all this testimony you're going to hear."*

He spoke with an attitude as if to dismiss and discredit everything that was said by the prosecutor.

Defense: *"Well the testimony that they constantly reiterate is dissembled, fabricated and flat out lies. And the reason they want you to solely rely on the fabricated testimony is to divert your attention away from one simple fact. THEY HAVE NO EVIDENCE!*

"They have no proof that my clients made any credit cards. They have no proof that my clients ran any real estate scam. In fact, you will hear honest and truthful testimony that during the hours the real estate offices were open my clients were at work. This has been proven and you'll see that," he said in a nonchalant tone.

"These alleged murders that they're asking you to believe in, they have no forensic evidence for ladies and gentleman. They have no fingerprints to match any of my clients. They have no weapons. They have no DNA matching any of my clients. Better yet THEY HAVE NO BODIES! Not one crime scene has been found where these so called murders took place. Scientific evidence doesn't lie. But people do. Scientific evidence doesn't have motive, ladies and gentleman.

"So what does the State have to rely on to support these allegations? The hope that a jury will be naïve enough to believe in a bunch of fabricated stories they intend to pass off as honest testimony. The problem with that is this. From the very first orders issued by the detectives who handled this case and you'll hear from them I'm sure, they were concerned more with their own images and the publicity that might be generated from this case as well as the recognition that they would receive if they could get these cases closed. They didn't care about doing real police work and upholding the oath that they took as officers. They wanted nothing more than to be in the limelight. They're not here looking for justice for the people that were affected by these allegations and you will hear honest testimony from one of their own about exactly that.

"You'll hear how these detectives trampled through witnesses, how they made cold statements about not caring about the fact

that they had no forensic evidence to link my clients to any of this. All they cared was that they were up for a promotion if they could get this conviction.

"Ladies and gentleman of the jury, this case was built on arrogance and deceit. Hearsay and a small amount of circumstantial evidence and nothing more is what the State will present to you. The defense will prove that Jada Cruz, Solace Ford and Angel Washington had no involvement in any realty scam, no involvement in the credit card and counterfeit money scams, and certainly no involvement in any drug trafficking or murders and disappearances. Thank you."

Reporter: "That was heavy stuff from both the prosecution and the defense. Joining me right now is former prosecutor David Banning. Welcome, David."

Mr. Banning: "Thank you, Lori. Heavy indeed. I think the strongest statement made was that forensic evidence can't lie but people can. That has to be something that sticks out in the minds of the jurors."

Reporter: "Absolutely, David. Based on your experience do you think the prosecution will be able to get away from the fact that they have no forensic evidence?"

Mr. Banner: "I think it definitely poses somewhat of a challenge, but many of cases were tried and won with just circumstantial evidence, Lori. I think it's a matter of how strong the testimonies from their witnesses are."

Reporter: "And we heard how defense attorney Edward Pacatino feels about that."

Mr. Banner: "Well, Pacatino is known for trying to discredit the prosecution as well as the witnesses. That's his style and so far it's kept him at the top of the game."

Reporter: "I, for one, can't wait to see how this all pans out. It's the battle of the best vs. the best in this one. Thanks for joining us, David."

Mr. Banner: "Thanks for having me, Lori."

Reporter: "We're going to take break for a moment but please continue to join us on *The Best Defense* as we cover the trial of the "Pennsylvania Queen Pins.""

We attentively listened to see who was coming out first for the prosecution. Mr. Pacatino told them the names on the witness list, but now they were able to put a face to the names. We were eager to find out who knew or thought they knew anything about us.

State: "The prosecution would like to call Angela Steinbach to the stand."

Lace, Angel and I all looked at each other as if to say "*who the fuck is she?*" We were sure we didn't know her so we shrugged our shoulders and listened to her get sworn in to tell the truth.

State: "Good morning, Ms. Steinbach. Can you begin by telling us why you're here?"

Witness: "Well a few years ago, I saw an ad in the paper for some townhouses being built. I responded to the ad and went down to the company to put in an application."

State: "What happened when you got there?"

Witness: "I remember filling out some papers and the girl making copies of my I.D. and pay stubs. I also gave them a money order for a thousand dollars as a deposit for when the house was ready."

State: "And how long were you told it would take?"

Witness: "I was told two months."

State: "So did you move in after the two months was up?"

Witness: "No. After the two months was up, I tried to call the office to find out what happened but the number was disconnected."

State: "Did you try to reach the office another way?"

Witness: "Yes. I went down to the place I put the application in at but it was closed down."

State: "What did you do when you found out they were closed?"

Witness: "I called four-one-one and requested a listing for them under the company name but they had none."

State: "Was that all?"

Witness: "No. I also went to one of the houses that was done and spoke with a tenant there."

State: "And what did you learn?"

Witness: "I found out that she went to a different then where I went to rent the house. She took me to the right place after I had explained to her what happened and the people there told me that they didn't have any other offices and they had been getting the same complaint from different people for months."

State: "Did they tell you how to resolve the issue?"

Witness: "They told me they believed it was a scam someone was doing but I could put in a real application with them if I was still interested."

State: "And did you put in that application, Ms. Steinbach?"

Witness: "No. They told me the process was correct that the scammers were using and they required a $1000 deposit. I didn't have it."

State: "What happened as a result of you being scammed?"

Witness: "Well I gave notice to my landlord that I was moving thirty days in advance like I was required. He agreed to let me live out my security for that apartment for my last month there. When I found out it was all a scam I was still required to move out because of the notice I gave. I was told that if I was going to stay I would need to pay the security deposit again as well as two months' rent because they already had someone new to rent the apartment."

State: "Did you move or pay the fees to stay?"

Witness: "I'm a single mother with a disabled child. I didn't have the money to pay all the fees so I had to move out."

State: "And where did you go?"

Witness: "Well for the first thirty days we stayed at a shelter. Then I called a friend and asked could we stay there for a while and they said yes. So we stayed there until I was able to afford to move again."

State: *"Have you moved since then?"*

Witness: *"Yes. That was years ago. I've moved since then."*

State: *"Ok, just checking. Ms. Steinbach, I know it was a long time ago but do you remember what the girl at the office looked like where you put in the application?"*

Witness: *"Yes. I think so."*

State: *"Is she in this courtroom today?"*

Witness: *"Yes."*

State: *"Can you please point her out for us?"*

Witness: *"She is sitting there with the tan suit on."*

State: *"Your Honor, please let the record reflect that the witness has identified Angel Washington as the person from the office. No further questions."*

Judge: *"Would the defense like to cross?"*

Defense: *"Of course, Your Honor."*

Defense: *"Ms. Steinbach, is it?"*

Witness: *"Yes."*

Defense: *"You stated that you think you can identify the person from the office. Are you sure about the person you pointed out?"*

Witness: *"Well it has been some years, but it looks to be her. Just much older."*

Defense: *"Ms. Steinbach, do you wear corrective eye care?"*

Witness: *"Yes I do."*

Defense: *"You're not wearing glasses today so it's safe to assume that you're wearing corrective contact lenses correct?"*

Witness: *"Well not at the moment. I ripped one of them and I need to buy new ones so I'm not wearing any at the moment."*

Defense: *"You're not wearing any?"*

Witness: *"No. I'm not. But I can still see okay."*

Defense: *"Ms. Steinbach...the defendant you pointed out is about fifteen to twenty- feet away. Are you sure you don't want to take a closer look?"*

Witness: *"No. I can see her just fine."*

Defense: *"Ok. We'll move on. You were recently involved in a motor vehicle accident were you not?"*

Witness: *"Yes but I don't see what that has to do with any-thing."*

Defense: *"Please just answer the questions yes or no. Now you filed a suit against the other party involved in that accident is that correct?"*

State: *"Objection, Your Honor. This line of questioning has no bearing."*

Defense: *"Your Honor, I'm trying to establish the witnesses' reliability when it comes to her vision."*

Judge: *"Overruled. I'll allow it."*

Defense: *"Do you need me to repeat the question, Ms. Stein-bach?"*

Witness: *"No. The answer is yes, I sued them."*

Defense: *"And can you tell us the outcome of that case."*

Witness: *"It was determined that I was actually at fault be-cause I wasn't wearing any glasses or lenses."*

Defense: *"So is it safe to say that your vision is not reliable without some sort of correction?"*

Witness: *"I can see just fine. I can see better with them, but I can see just fine and that looks like the person who was there at that office to me."*

Defense: *"Are you one hundred percent sure it's the same person?"*

Witness: *"I'm almost positive."*

Defense: *"Well unfortunately, Ms. Steinbach, in a court of law, almost doesn't count. No further questions for this witness, Your Honor."*

The prosecutor called several more witnesses and they all had a story to tell about how they were scammed. I think the prosecutor intentionally tracked down the people with the worst stories. I find it hard to believe that a measly one thousand dollars caused so many problems for people.

One lady said she was living in her car for three months because of it. A man said his wife kicked him out the house because she thought he was lying about where the money went because he had a gambling problem.

An elderly lady got up there and said she was renting the house for her granddaughter who was trying to get her kids back from the state. She said her only source of income was social security benefits and she had been saving a little each month until she finally had the grand. She said her granddaughter was a recovering addict and had been doing so much better and was finally ready to start a new life. She only made minimum wage and needed some help until she found a better job. She cried on the stand when she told the part of not being able to get the kids because she was scammed out of the money and an affordable apartment.

One by one the prosecutor called them out and Mr. Pacatino fought to discredit their testimony. He found something on each of them to use as the real reason why they had the misfortunes they did.

He asked the elderly lady if it were true that the real reason her granddaughter didn't get the kids back was because she relapsed on drugs and not because of the apartment.

He asked the guy who was kicked out, wasn't the real reason because he did in fact, gamble away the money that was supposed to be for the new furniture as well the money his wife gave him to pay off a credit card bill.

He asked the lady who lived out of her car wasn't it true that she was paid by the detectives to come in and testify. He told of how she already was living in her car when they found her and offered her money to come in. He said she was told exactly what to say on the stand. The lady started crying when Mr. Pacatino began to shout at her saying that she's committing perjury and could go to jail for it.

The prosecutor called for an objection stating that the defense was badgering the witness and the judge sustained it.

It didn't matter to Mr. Pacatino, he tried to make them all look like a bunch of liars on the stand and it worked. The first day was surely a crazy one, but the girls soon learned that it was only the beginning.

Reporter: "It's day four of the trial in the case of the Pennsylvania Queen Pins. Everyone is making their way back into the courtroom after the judge called an hour recess for lunch. This morning you heard testimony from some of the people who had their credit card information stolen. This afternoon the prosecution has three more witnesses lined up, one of whom includes a Manager at Best Buy, a popular electronics store, who says these girls were definitely living the Luxurious Life. Let's go back into the court room as the Best Defense continues."

Judge: *"Is the prosecution ready to proceed?"*

State: *"Yes we are your honor. The prosecution would like to call Miguel Santos to the stand."*

By now I knew that we didn't know any of these people so I no longer tried to figure out who they were. We just watched as the short Hispanic guy took the stand with his khaki pants hanging slightly off of him and his light blue shirt. When he sat down Angel winked at him when he looked in her direction. He put his head down and smiled.

State: *"Mr. Santos can you please tell us what you do for a living?"*

Witness: *"I'm a manger at a Best Buy store in Philly."*

State: *"And by Philly you mean Philadelphia?"*

Witness: *"Yeah, sorry."*

State: *"How long have you been manager at Best Buy?"*

Witness: *"I been working there for eight years and I been a manger for seven."*

State: *"So you were managing at this location back in 2002?"*

Witness: *"Yes, I was."*

State: *"Can you tell us how you came about knowing the defendants?"*

Witness: *"Well they regularly shopped in the store."*

State: *"And did you assist them when they came in?"*

Witness: *"Well not exactly. They were known for making large purchases and anything over a certain amount needed a manager to turn the key at the register."*

State: *"So, you would be the one to approve the purchase?"*

Witness: *"Yes."*

State: *"And what sort of things would they buy?"*

Witness: *"Well it varied, but it was usually things like plasma televisions, high- tech stereo systems, computers, digital cameras and stuff like that."*

State: *"So lots of electronics?"*

Witness: *"Yes. Mostly."*

State: *"Would you say that they purchased more electronics than the average person?"*

Defense: *"Objection your honor. The witness is not an expert on how much electronics a person buys."*

Judge: *"Sustained."*

State: *"Mr. Santos, in your opinion did the defendants purchase more electronics than any other customer you dealt with?"*

Witness: *"Yes. I would say so. They were definitely living the luxurious life. They only bought the best and lots of it."*

State: *"No further questions. Your witness."*

Mr. Pacatino stood up and slowly approached the witness. He looked to be in deep thought about something.

Defense: *"Mr. Santos, you said you remember the defendants from 2002 correct?"*

Witness: *"Yes."*

Defense: *"How can you be so sure about the year?"*

Witness: *"Well, I was just finishing up my last year of school and like I said they shopped there all the time."*

Defense: *"Is it true, Mr. Santos, that the real reason you remember so well is because both Jada Cruz and Angel Washington declined your offers for a date to a graduation party?"*

Witness: *"No."*

Defense: *"No, that's not the reason or no, they never declined your offers?"*

Witness: *"Well I asked them out a couple of times, but that's not the reason."*

Defense: *"Isn't it true, Mr. Santos, that you had a huge crush on Angel Washington and whenever you saw her in the store you would rush over to help her?"*

Witness: *"No, I mean, well yes, but that's because I knew she always spent a lot of money and I would have to go over there anyway to turn to the key, like I said."*

Defense: *"Mr. Santos, when customers make a credit card purchase are they required to show you identification?"*

Witness: *"Yes."*

Defense: *"When you came over to turn the key as you state, did you ask the defendant for identification?"*

Witness: *"Yes. I always ask for ID."*

Defense: *"In fact, Mr. Santos, that's how you came to know Angel's name isn't it? You learned her name by looking at her ID?"*

Witness: *"I don't think so. I'm sure she told me herself."*

Defense: *"You're sure she told you her name herself?"*

Witness: *"Yes."*

Defense: *"Ok...let me get this straight, she told you her name herself and you always check ID, correct."*

Witness: *"Yes."*

Defense: *"Is that the same for the other two defendants as well?"*

Witness: *"Yes. I believe so."*

Defense: *"You could lose your job if you didn't check for proper identification for such large purchases that were made on a daily basis correct?"*

Witness: *"Yes, I suppose I could."*

Defense: *"So, if they told you their names, Mr. Santos, and you did your job by checking for proper identification, than it's safe to say that they were making purchases with their own credit cards. Is that not correct?"*

Witness: *"Well I don't know. I mean they... M-m-aybe they didn't."*

Defense: *"Well, did they tell you a different name each time they came in and showed a different ID each time they came in?"*

Witness: *"They could've. I don't remember."*

Defense: *"Well just a few moments ago you were certain about these things, Mr. Santos. Which is it? Did they or didn't they tell you their names when you asked them out, and did you or didn't you check for proper identification to match the names you were given?"*

State: *"Objection. He's asking the witness multiple questions at once, Your Honor."*

Judge: *"Sustained. Please ask one question at a time and wait for the witness to respond."*

Defense: *"No need. No further questions for this witness."*

The prosecution called another person whose credit card information was stolen and another person who claimed to manage a store that we shopped at. Mr. Pacatino didn't have too much on them, so his cross-examinations had little or no impact.

The prosecution finally was able to put some convincing witnesses on the stand. Mr. Pacatino assured us that they still had nothing. He said they still hadn't done anything to get us a conviction so we were hopeful.

The following day the prosecution called five more witnesses to testify about the credit cards. They even had a witness that said they bought things regularly from us. One girl told how she furnished her whole apartment by telling us what she wanted and how we went out and got it and charged her half price. Mr. Pacatino tore her to pieces on the stand.

The other witnesses were more people who had their information stolen and one person who worked for the credit card company. The man told of all the complaint's they received from customers about the charges to their cards. He told about the investigations they did through their fraud department. The prosecution even had a tape of what looked like me in a clothing store making a purchase. My hair was different and I had on sunglasses. It wasn't apparent that it was me but the prosecution argued that it was in fact, "Jada Cruz" in disguise at the store. The woman had the same body structure as me. The man got the tape from the store when the company did an investigation on one of the claims.

Mr. Pacatino argued on cross that it was no way to determine that it was me in that video because you couldn't see the persons face at all. He said it would be easy to find someone with a figure that closely resembled mine and say it's me, but the fact is, the video was inconclusive because there was no way to positively identify the person in the video as being me.

When the witness left the stand it was pretty much up in the air as to whether or not his testimony and the video would stick or not. When they were done for the day we were happy. We were tired of sitting there listening to people trying to put us away for life.

Lace whispered to me that if we were on the streets, half these people would've been done already.

"Man, we never killed nobody wit' out a good reason," I whispered back. "These people wouldn't have posed a threat to us so why kill 'em?"

"And you don't think them testifying against us poses a threat?"

"I mean everybody we killed was in the game in some way or another. It was fair game. These just innocent people who stand to gain somethin' from all this. So fuck 'em. Mr. Pacatino, killing they asses anyway."

"Yeah I guess you right," Lace whispered back. "But fuck that, I would've killed them whether they in the game or not. Dead men can't tell any tales."

We laughed as the officers took us to the holding room until it was time for us to be taken back to the jail.

JADA

B y the end of the second week of the trial the prosecution was doing some serious damage. They had called several witnesses to testify about the counterfeit money scam. They had some of the people who bought it from us testify that they definitely bought it from us.

They told how they called to place orders and meeting locations were set up where they picked it up. They told how much it cost and why they bought it. The prosecutor showed a few bills to the jury and entered it as evidence.

Pacatino tried his hardest on cross to discredit the witnesses. He bought up the fact that one person must've been paid to testify because no one would incriminate them selves for nothing. He called a few other witnesses on previous crimes they were arrested for and argued that they had an agreement with the state to have the records removed if they testified. When he was done, he was clearly aggravated with the way things were going.

By the time the first detective took the stand, Pacatino and his team was huddled together going over notes. They were supposed to be whispering but it was evident that Pacatino was upset with them about something.

"I don't care! Go get it now!" He said loud enough for everyone to hear.

The guy got up, and left out the courtroom. Jada leaned in and asked was everything okay and Pacatino waved his hand and said, "Its fine."

The prosecutor questioned the first detective for more than an hour. He asked him about how he came to know of the crimes being committed by the defendants and how he went about investigating the information he received. He stated that it took them about two years to gather enough information to finally charge us.

He said they followed us for quite some time to various locations they believed we were meeting to sell drugs. The prosecution entered all the pictures the detectives had into evidence. He advised that all the other scams took place years ago so that's what took most of time. They were trying to gather the information for those crimes.

When Pacatino cross-examined the detective he asked to use the pictures. He went through each of them and asked the detectives to point out where in the picture the defendant is seen with drugs. Some pictures were of Lace going into a hotel with a duffel bag. Others were of Angel or me going into different places with nothing in our hands and leaving out with bags. Pacatino pointed out that it was assumptious to presume that drugs were in any of the bags.

Defense: *"Did you pull over any of their vehicles when you followed them?"*

Detective: *"No we did not."*

Defense: *"Detective, if you're tailing someone who you believe to be trafficking drugs, wouldn't it be wise to pull that vehicle over and check for the drugs?"*

Detective: *"Not in all cases. We were trying to build a case and we needed as much as evidence as possible. Busting them on the first chance we got wouldn't have helped us to do that."*

Defense: *"Detective, in the indictment it's stated that my clients sold kilo's at a time. Would it not be enough evidence to catch them with these kilos in their possession?"*

Detective: *"Yes, but we believed the more evidence we had to show that this wasn't a one-time thing, the better it would be for our case."*

Defense: *"Better for your case, huh? Detective, did you or anyone else from your department ever find drugs in my client's possession?"*

Detective: *"No not technically, we have the pictures of what has to be them transporting drugs and money as well witnesses who will testify that that's what was in the bags."*

Defense: *"I'm not asking about any witness at the moment, detective. I'm asking if you ever found any drugs in any one of my clients' possession."*

Detective: *"No, we did not."*

Defense: *"In fact, Detective, the day my clients were arrested you and your team had a search warrant, correct?"*

Detective: *"Yes, we did. We had a warrant for the home they all shared together as well as the apartment rental they had outside of that."*

Defense: *"And I assume your search team did a thorough search of both premises, correct?"*

Detective: *"Yes, we did."*

Defense: *"And were there any drugs, at either location?"*

Detective: *"No."*

Defense: *"How about weapons. Did you find any weapons there?"*

Detective: *"No, none."*

Defense: *"Did you find any credit cards or counterfeit money during your search?"*

Detective: *"No, it appeared that they knew we were coming and had cleared everything from both places."*

Defense: *"How can you determine that, detective?"*

Detective: *"Because we had specific information from our informant that certain things would be there, including the drugs and none of that was present."*

Defense: *"Could it be that you received false information from your informant, detective?"*

Detective: *"No. We believe the information is true and accurate and the defendants got rid of it all before we got there."*

Defense: *"Detective, we all know unless you're able to prove what you feel to be true a person shouldn't be charged with a crime correct?"*

Detective: *"Well, we feel as though the evidence and testimony of our witnesses is enough to prove our case, however, that's up to a jury to decide whether or not we've done so. Not me."*

Pacatino looked behind him to see if the guy he told to go get something had gotten back yet. When he saw that he hadn't he looked frustrated?

Defense: "No further questions at the moment for this witness. However, the defense would like to be able to re-call this witness at a later time, Your Honor."

The detective looked at the Judge for his response. The Judge stated that he could be recalled and the Detective stepped down.

Judge: "Is the prosecution ready to proceed with their next witness?"

State: "We would like to request a short recess before preceding, Your Honor."

Judge: "Okay. We'll take a fifteen minute recess."

Angel stood up to stretch her legs and Lace did the same. I whispered that I was gonna ask for us to use the restroom. Pacatino was off to the side talking with the other attorney when I motioned for him to come over. When I told him we needed to use the restroom he had the officer come and escort us to the back. The officer stood outside while we went in.

"Yo, I don't know what's going on but Pacatino trippin'," said Lace.

"I heard the other guy say something about leavin' the pictures at the office," said Angel. "That's when Pacatino got mad."

"Oh, it had to be some pictures of that detective doing somethin' shady then," I said.

"Well I hope they get 'em. That will help us a lot," said Lace.

"I'm sure he got it under control," I said. "Come on, let's go before they come in lookin' for us."

"Where the hell we gon' run to?" Lace said laughing. "It ain't even no windows up in this muthafucka."

We all laughed and went out the door. When we got back to the courtroom, we saw that the guy had returned and Pacatino was looking through a folder that had pictures in it.

"Yo. It definitely looks like some pictures he lookin at," I said. We took our seats and waited for the judge to return.

When the prosecution called the next detective to the stand, his story was almost identical to the other guys. The only difference was he said he actually wanted to stop us on many different occasions when they followed us, but he had orders from the lead detective not too.

On cross-examination Pacatino grabbed his folder that held the pictures in it.

Defense: *"Detective, at any point during your investigation did you attempt to bribe anyone to come in as a witness for the state?"*

Detective: *"No. Not ever. Those allegations are ridiculous."*

Defense: *"I don't need to remind you that you're under oath, detective. Correct?"*

Detective: *"I know I'm under oath...my answer is still no. We led an honest investigation."*

Defense: *"Detective, isn't it true that you and your team were getting so frustrated during the last few months that things weren't going the way you hoped, that you made a comment about being able to buy the proof you needed?"*

Detective: *"No. I never made such comments to anyone."*

Defense: *"Detective, may I ask that you take a look at these photos for a moment, Your Honor, may I approach the witness?"*

Judge: *"Let me see the photos first and then show the prosecutor before doing so."*

Pacatino showed them all the photos. The prosecutor looked shocked when he saw them. He put his head down and handed the photo's back to Pacatino. He handed the pictures to the detective who immediately began rubbing the top of his baldhead.

Detective: *"Where did you get these?"*

Defense: *"I'll ask the questions, detective."*

Defense: *"Detective, the photographs are marked one through four. Can you tell me whether or not you're in all four photos?"*

Detective: *"Yeah I'm in the pictures."*

Defense: *"And who else can you identify in the pictures marked with the numbers two and four on them?"*

The detective stalled for a minute before responding. When he did it was barely audible.

Defense: *"Can you please speak loud and clear, detective? We can't hear you.*

Detective: *"It's myself and Detective Rogers in the photographs along with another gentleman."*

Defense: *"Yourself and Detective Rogers that we just heard from a short while ago, correct?"*

Detective: *"Yes."*

The detective answered in an irate tone. He looked like he was ready to beat the hell out of Pacatino.

Defense: *"Can you please take a look at the pictures marked one and three and identify the parties in those pictures?"*

Detective: *"It's myself, Detective Rogers, and another gentleman."*

Defense: *"Detective, in those photos, it clearly shows you handing the other gentleman an envelope. Can you please tell the court what's in that envelope?"*

Detective: *"I don't remember. It could've been some evidence of some sort."*

Defense: *"Or it could've been five-thousand dollars, Detective."*

Detective: *"You're out of your mind."*

Defense: *"Am I?"*

Detective: *"Yes. What you're suggesting is crazy."*

Defense: *"Your Honor, I would like to enter into evidence these photographs along with this envelope containing five thousand dollars in it."*

State: *"Objection. How can we be certain that it's the same envelope with the same contents as what's in those photo's. This is absurd, Your Honor."*

Defense: *"Your Honor, we have enhanced photos of the envelope seen in those photographs. There are very distinctive words and writing on the top of the envelope as well as you can see the money sticking out of the envelope."*

Judge: *"Counselors, please approach for a side bar".*

The prosecutor and the defense went over to a huddle with the Judge. No one knew what was being said over there. Me, Angel and Lace looked at each other with a smirk on our faces.

"Got his ass now," said Lace.

When they were done the Judge ruled that the photos could be entered in as evidence and instructed Pacatino to continue with his line of questioning.

Defense: *"Detective, this envelope was retrieved from the gentleman seen in the photos with you and detective Rogers. Can you please explain why you were handing him an envelope with five thousand dollars in it if you weren't trying to bribe him to testify?"*

Detective: *"We weren't bribing anybody. I was paying off a gambling debt. That's all."*

Defense: *"Detective, the gentleman in the photo...was he not a member of your unit?"*

Detective: *"Yes, he was."*

Defense: *"And what happened to him?"*

State: *"Objection, Your Honor, the detective is not on trial here."*

Judge: *"Over ruled. Please answer the question."*

Detective: *"He was found dead in his apartment."*

Defense: *"And do you know what the cause of death was?"*

Detective: *"A gunshot wound to the head."*

Defense: *"Isn't it true, detective, that this officer was killed because he refused to cooperate with your team and provide false testimony during this trial!"*

State: *"Objection, Your Honor."*

Detective: *"He was killed, but we didn't have anything to do with his death!"*

Judge: *"Objection sustained. Please withdraw the witness' response to that question. You're treading on thin-ice, counselor."*

Defense: *"Sorry, Your Honor. No further questions."*

I looked over at Lace and Angel. I knew exactly who was responsible for that detective's death. Yeah, they tried to bribe him and he refused but they didn't kill him. Rubin had him killed for not telling him about the investigation until the last minute. The cop wasn't going to go against Rubin and testify against the girls no matter how much they tried to pay him. But he made the terrible mistake of not telling him sooner so he paid with his life.

I loved how Pacatino made it look like the detectives killed him. Either way they were crooked. They knew a lot but had no way of proving it so they got grimy. They were getting what they deserved as far as I was concerned.

Back in the holding cell I told the other girls about my thoughts on the matter.

"Yo, that shit worked out perfectly in the court room too."

"Hell yeah, I forgot you told us Rubin had the cop killed. The lawyer just flipped that shit all around," Lace whispered. "I love this guy."

"How y'all think he got them pictures though?" Angel asked.

"I don't know and I don't care, girl. I'm just glad he got 'em," said Lace. "We gon' beat this thing wit' flying colors."

"I hope you right, girl. I hope you right," said Angel shaking her head.

JADA

When I got in my cell I noticed a letter was waiting for me on my bunk. I picked it up real fast not knowing who would be sending me mail. I had been locked up for almost nine months and no letters came for me. We would get food packages and other supplies we needed as well as money in our commissary every week but no letters. We knew the packages and money came from Zy and Rubin, but I wondered who was sending the letter.

I knew it had to be one of the crooked guards who were on the payroll that got this to me. I sat on the bottom bunk and looked at the writing on the envelope. It had no return address on it but I knew it had to be from Zy when I saw the beautiful penmanship on it. We always complimented Zy on how pretty her handwriting was.

I tore open the letter and began to read.

Dear Jada,

Please forgive me for not writing sooner. I'm sure you know why though. You were the one who taught me stuff like that. I've been sending y'all any and everything that's allowed and making sure y'all had all the dough you needed in there. I know it doesn't change much but I hope it helps. Anyway, I know I'm not supposed to be writing y'all but I had to this one time.

I have some shit to tell you. I sent this over night to make sure you got it in time and I sent ya lawyer a letter 2 days ago. But Rubin is really sick. He is dying girl and I don't know how but he contacted me. He asked me to fly out to meet with him because he had some very important information that you needed to know. He

154

wanted to be the one to tell you in person but unfortunately he is now bedridden. He asked that I send you this letter for him.

Jada ,there is no easy way to say any of this so I'ma just tell you. Rubin asked me to tell you that he is sorry for all the pain that he has caused you. He said that your father was working for him since he was in high school and he never met anyone more loyal. He remembered when your dad first came to him and told him that he had a new girl friend and one day she would be his wife. Rubin let him use one of his brand new cars to take her out on their first date. He said he never knew a man more in love with a woman than your father was with your mother.

When he found out he was about to be a father he was ecstatic and wanted to marry ya mother right away. Rubin said he told him he would pay for the wedding after he finished school. So once they graduated, he did just that. He said he felt like a proud father watching his only son marry the love of his life.

Here's the hard part Jada, so please, brace ya'self. He said on the night that your father was supposed to pick up and deliver the goods he never showed. It wasn't like him at all. He never did anything like that before. He didn't even call him and tell him what happened. Rubin said other guys were already making claims that ya father was cheating him. He said a lot of shipments were coming up short and ya dad was the only one tryna get out the game at the time. He said when another one of his loyal workers came back and told him that it was ya father who took the stuff and he didn't know what to do. He said if he was to let him live then it could jeopardize his own empire. He felt that others would have taken him to be soft and tried the same thing. It was either lose a son or lose his respect. He believed at the time that all a man had was his respect so he ordered for him to be killed.

Jada, he said that it wasn't until about two years before he finally met you that he learned the truth about what really happened to that shipment. He said he was devastated to learn that it was all a set up and your father had not crossed him.

He told me that he has lived with the hurt and pain all this time and the burden of it was killing him quicker that the cancer. He wanted desperately to meet you after that. He felt like he owed you the world for taking away your parents.

He decided that no matter what it cost him, he would die trying to make things right. That's why he did all that he has for you. He asked me to tell you from the bottom of his soul that he is sorry. He knows there is no way to right the wrong because nothing could bring them back. But he couldn't leave this earth without telling you the truth. He sends all his love and heartfelt apologies Jada and asked that you find it somewhere in your heart to forgive him.

I dropped the letter as the tears poured down my face. I screamed out in pain from what I had just read. I screamed and threw things around the small cell. I shattered the mirror with my fist before dropping to my knees and sobbing loudly. I folded the letter up and didn't even finish reading it.

The next day in the holding cell while waiting for the trial to resume, I handed the letter to Lace and Angel while tears ran down my face.

"What's wrong, Jada?"

"Tell us what happened?" Lace screamed.

I couldn't control my tears long enough to get anything out. Angel began to read. She tapped Lace and showed it to her before continuing. She dropped the letter at almost the same point as I did, neither of them being able to continue reading.

The tears slowly poured down Angel's face as she too felt my pain. We held each other until I stopped crying. Lace wet two face towels and handed it to us.

"This muthafucka pretending to be a friend of my father's," I screamed. "I sat in the house of my parent's killer! I accepted everything he gave me! I can't believe I looked at this muthafucka like a father or grandfather or some shit!! A fuckin' mentor!! He had my parents killed," I screamed, and began to cry even harder.

Angel held on to me and silently cried with me. She could only imagine what I was feeling. Lace picked up the letter and read it all the way through. When she got passed the part about Rubin killing my parents, she knew neither Angel nor me could've read the letter in its entirety. What she read was unbelievable.

SYMONE

I tossed and turned all night listening to the sounds of the crickets outside my bedroom window. Tomorrow was the big day and the more I thought about what I was about to do, the more I wanted to throw up.

I was scared shitless but I knew that it was no turning back now. I opened my mouth and sang a whole fuckin' album to those feds when they cornered me. I mean yeah we were all friends, but it was either them or me.

Twenty-five years to life or no time at all. I tried to get Jada to understand how bad I needed the coke connect but she was so caught up tryna be the fuckin' boss of it all that she wasn't hearing me.

They didn't even want us. They wanted the muthafucka who was sending all this shit to the U.S. All we had to do was give him up and we would've been clear. I admit…I did have a few small other ulterior motives for wanting to get to the connect, but after they cornered me, the main reason became to avoid prison.

I turned over and looked at the clock for what had to be the tenth time since I went to bed. It read three-thirty am. *Damn, wasn't it three o'clock, three hours ago?* Time definitely had to be at a standstill. Maybe it thought it was helping me out, but it was killing me, dragging like that.

I got up and went to look in the living room. The fat fuck assigned to make sure I stayed safe was in a coma on my couch. I looked through the peephole and the other cop was fighting sleep reading the newspaper. *Shit. I could do a better job of protecting my dam self,* I thought.

I climbed back in the bed, lay on my side as I pulled the cover over my head hoping it would help me sleep. The last thing I needed was to be tired on the stand. I let the sound of the crickets soothe my thoughts and ease my mind as I fell back into a much needed deep sleep, only to be awakened a short while later by the sound of my door being kicked in. I heard the gunshots and my body froze on the bed as if the mattress would be my savior. I knew this place they chose for me wasn't gonna be safe. I know these girls and I knew that they would eventually find out it was me and if they did, I was gonna wish I was dead for real.

They must've sent somebody here to take care of me. I tried to fight my thoughts off knowing there was no room for me to entertain them at the moment. *How the fuck am I gonna get out of here?*

JADA

I grabbed the letter from Lace and ripped it up.

"Noooooo, Jada," Lace yelled out. "Y'all didn't read all of it!! Don't you know that…"

"Don't say another word about it, Lace. I'm not keeping this fuckin' letter. It will haunt me for the rest of my days," I said, fighting to talk through the tears.

"I know, Jada, but you gotta listen to me!!"

"Let it go, Lace, don't you see how upset she is?" said Angel.

"I'm tryna tell y'all somethin' important though that was in that letter if y'all would just listen!" Lace screamed.

"Well what is it? What's so fuckin' important that you're forcing me to do what I don't want to do? Huh?"

"Symone ain't fuckin' dead!" Lace yelled. "She ain't dead!"

JADA

M r. Pacatino was furious at the letter he received. He had no idea that it was a possibility that the other girl could still be alive. He would've never overlooked the matter if he thought for one second she wasn't actually dead. He knew it could mean the case if he didn't do something fast. He needed all the details from us so he set up a visit right away.

Even though the Judge had agreed that it would be a violation of the amendment to keep the witness' identity concealed, he did allow the identity of the witness to remain confidential up until the point of their testimony for safety reasons.

When he got to the jail it was a little after midnight. We girls were escorted in the room and the correctional officer removed our handcuffs. Me and Angel's eyes were puffy and he could tell we had been crying for a long time.

"I thought we had an agreement?!" he yelled. "I thought I stressed how important it was that the three of you leave no stones unturned or it could cost us?!!"

"We didn't tell you about our other friend because we wanted to make sure she stayed out of it," I said. "But we didn't know she was still alive."

"Make sure she stayed out of it?!" He repeated in anger. "You wanted to make sure she stayed out of it?!" he screamed again. "Maybe you don't understand the seriousness of these charges. Or, maybe you don't care that you could spend the rest of your pretty little lives in jail. Am I the only one who cares about that?" He asked looking around the room at the three of us.

"Of course we care," said Lace.

"Then why would you not tell me about her?!!"

We were quiet. Besides, there was nothing we could say to change the fact that we fucked up.

"Okay, let's start this from the beginning. I want you to tell me everything this Symone girl knows."

"She knows it all," said Angel. "Everything that was done, she was there from the beginning and a part of it all."

"What made you think she was dead?" He asked.

I told him about the phone call I received the day we all went to dinner.

"What was the detective's name you spoke with?" he asked continuing to take notes.

"He said his name was Detective umm …. Damn, I don't remember. I know he said he was with Homicide," I said.

"And he wanted you to come down and identify the body and you didn't?"

"No we didn't go. We wasn't on good terms at the time because she was stealing from us and her and her brother was doing their own thing with our product so honestly we was gon' kill her ourselves until we got that call," said Lace. "So, when they told us she was dead we didn't wanna have nuthin else to do wit' it."

"Detective Rogers," I yelled. "That was his name!!"

"Wait a minute," said Pacatino dropping his pencil. "You're saying the detective that told you she was dead was Rogers?"

"Yeah, that's what he said on the phone."

"Jada, that's the same Roger's that testified. Did you not realize that?" he snapped

"No, I didn't," I snapped back.

"Okay. Okay. Let's calm down for a minute here. We're all on the same team." Pacatino looked frustrated. "Well it looks like they were pretty sure y'all wouldn't want to come down and identify the body if she already suspected y'all knew she was stealing and planned on killing her anyway. They just said that to make it look good. To get you all to believe that she was actually dead."

"Look! Our friend Zy, who sent us the letter saying that Symone was still alive, said somethin' about Rubin finding out who the clean up guys were in her letter," said Lace. "Rubin already connected with them and told them what's coming. He pretty much let them know that Symone would do anything she could to protect herself, including giving them up. Now the main clean up guys aren't willing to come forward, but they have some dudes who are ready to take the bodies if they have to. Zy has all the information you need to put them on the stand."

"Yeah, but I don't see how that could possibly help you all if they worked for you," said Pacatino.

"Like I told you," I jumped in. "We never knew who they were. Symone was the one who handled that shit. The only one, at that. So we don't care if they're involved or not. Not if it will help us anyway."

"See!" Pacatino said jumping out his seat. "Now you're thinking like we play for the same team." He rummaged through his papers and found the notes he had with their information on it.

"And these guys were paid right? So they know the drill?"

"Yeah, she said the fall guys got like five million a piece to take care of their families with so they gonna do whatever you need them to do."

"Well it ain't really cheating, if they only worked for her now is it?" Pacatino laughed.

"Fuck the prosecution. They been putting all those lying ass mutha fuckas on the stand throughout the whole trial," said Lace. "It ain't gon' hurt for you to sweeten ya case a lil bit too."

Pacatino laughed. "Your right about that one."

We went over a few more details before Pacatino left. He told us tomorrow would be a little crazy and it was important that we showed no emotion towards Symone. He had it under control.

"The prosecution may think they're doing serious damage but she's their last witness and then it's our turn. So be cool in there tomorrow okay?"

We all agreed we would show no expression in the courtroom and the officer cuffed us and brought us back to our cells.

SYMONE

The sound of the alarm going off woke me from my night-mare. I was not killed like I thought I was. I sat up and looked around the room thankful I was still alive and well. My body was soaked in sweat and not my own blood so I sighed in relief. I gathered my things and got ready to shower.

It was a long three-hour drive back to Pennsylvania. I felt like a death-row inmate taking the walk that would seal his fate as opposed to going to testify. All sorts of things ran through my head. I wondered if the girls looked any different after two years and what will happen to me when this trial is over.

I would be the one that sent them to jail for life. I was sure they would try to have me killed. I've dreamt about it for years and it has become my biggest fear in life. But I had to do what I had to do for me and my brother.

I was tired but my nerves wouldn't allow me to sleep. I watch-ed the other cars drive by and wished I was in one of them. I wished I had their life no matter how fucked up they thought it was. Their biggest fear was probably not being able to pay for their kids' college tuition funds. That was nothing. Switch places with me. I tried to channel my thoughts away from the whole trial long enough to get through the ride with some sort of peace of mind.

JADA

Everyone sat patiently waiting for the judge to come out of his chambers. When he did everyone stood as instructed and then sat back down.

Judge: "Is everyone present and ready to begin?"

"Yes, Your Honor." Both sides replied.

Judge: "Please call your witness,"

State: "The prosecution would like to call Symone Mitchell to the stand."

Symone walked in the courtroom with her head held high. She didn't want to look afraid like she really was. After she was sworn in, she took a seat and looked over at us. If looks could kill she would've surely met her maker in that instant.

We locked our eyes on her. I know she felt all the anger, hurt and betrayal we felt for her through our cold stares. But to Symone's surprise, we all remained calm though. Symone was sure we would jump out their seats in a rage that she wasn't dead.

State: "Ms. Mitchell, can you please tell the court how you know the defendants?"

Symone: "I've known them for about six or seven years now. We use to be friends."

State: "And by friends what do you mean exactly? You hung out and went to the movies together?"

Symone: "Not just that. I lived with them and was a witness to everything they did."

State: "So you were roommates?"

Symone: "Correct."

State: "And were you roommates with them during the years 2001-2005?"

Symone: *"Yes, I was."*

State: *"Can you tell me what the defendants did for a living during that time?"*

Symone: *"When we first met, they worked for a telephone company."*

State: *"And did that soon change?"*

Symone: *"Yes."*

State: *"Do you know the circumstances in which it all changed?"*

Symone: *"It didn't change immediately. First, they decided to run a realty scam in which they set up several office locations and had people come in and fill out applications for homes. They charged each of them a thousand dollars."*

State: *"Did they ever rent the homes to the applicants?"*

Symone: *"No. Like I said, it was all a scam to make money."*

Pacatino took notes throughout Symone's four-hour testimony. She gave details of everything that was done. What she didn't do was admit that she was a part of it all. By the time the judge had called for a lunch recess we were on the edge of our seats. We wanted to kill her for what she was trying to do to us.

"Man, I don't know no more," said Angel. "This ain't lookin good right now. She is telling every single detail of what happened. The jury gon' know she telling the truth. How else could she be so descriptive wit' it? Maybe we should take a plea deal."

"Are you fuckin serious?" Lace snapped. "We ain't coppin' to shit because of this bitch. You already know Mr. Pacatino gon' handle it, so why you trippin?"

"I just didn't know she would say so much. I mean, I knew she was coming to testify but I didn't know she would make it seem like she wasn't wit' it. We gon' do life if we don't take a bargain now."

"We are not taking any plea deal, Angel!" I jumped in. "We all knew what we was facing when we started this whole trial so we not about to change our story in the middle of it. Why you so scared all of sudden?"

"I knew what I was facing when we started, but Symone was suppose to be dead."

"Man, you on some other shit right now," said Lace waving her hand.

"So what you gon' do, Angel? Go back out there and tell them you wanna cop a deal? If you do that then you make all of us look guilty," I said.

"I know. I know. I just don't know what to do y'all," Angel cried. "I just don't wanna spend the rest of my life in jail."

"We gon' get through this but you gotta remember what's important. We need to ride together right now. If one of us crumble then we all gon" crumble you know?" I said.

"Man, fuck all dat pampering shit! Angel you better shake that shit off right now cuz that coppin' out shit you talkin' makin' you look real weak right now. We gon' ride like we said we was. If we blow trial, then we blow trial, but I ain't coppin' to damn thing!"

"See…that pride right there is what's gon have us in this bitch forever!" Angel said angrily. "I ain't about to spend my whole life locked up! At least if we take a deal then we still got a chance of gettin' out one day!"

"Uuuggghh! I'm gettin' the hell out this bathroom before I forget who the fuck you are in here," said Lace as she flung open the door and left.

"It's gon' be aiight, ma. We just have to wait and see what our lawyer can do."

"By then it might be too late, Jada. Lace not gon' listen to me but she might listen to you. We gotta end this now."

The banging on the bathroom door startled us.

"Let's go, ladies!" Yelled the officer outside of the door.

"Just be cool a lil longer, Angel. I know you scared, all of us are. But we gotta be strong."

We walked out the bathroom together hoping that the other would do what we felt was the right thing collectively.

Symone went back on the stand after the lunch break. She hadn't even begun to tell them about all the drugs and murders. This part of her testimony would prove to be the most crucial. She went through every single murder with a fine-toothed comb. She even told about the day Zy and Angel were questioned about killing that guy who stole Angel's car. She spared nothing on the stand. She told all the details of how and why the guys were killed and where it all took place.

When she was asked what was done with the bodies, she lied and said I would make a call and some dudes came and cleaned up the mess and took the bodies. She said none of us ever knew where they took them. All we knew was the bodies never turned up.

It wasn't until two hours later that Pacatino got to cross-examine her. They only had two hours left for the day and she was the last witness for the prosecution and the most important. Pacatino knew he had his work cut out for him.

Defense: "*Ms. Mitchell, were you granted immunity for your testimony in this trial?*"

Symone: "*No I wasn't.*"

Pacatino shook his head in a yes motion as if to say okay. He looked at the prosecutor and smiled before continuing.

Defense: "*You said you've known my clients for about ten years, correct?*"

Symone: "*Yeah. About that.*"

Defense: "*You never said how you all met. Can you please tell us how you came to know the defendants?*"

Symone didn't expect that question. She quickly thought about whether or not she should tell the truth.

Symone: "*I met them at a job I worked at. They put in an application for a townhouse.*"

Defense: "*Did they ever move into that house?*"

Symone: "*No they didn't.*"

Defense: "*So, can you tell us how the friendship came about?*"

Symone: "*Like any other I guess. We talked that day and exchanged numbers and it just developed from there.*"

Defense: "*Is that so? Ms. Mitchell, we've listened to you testify, under oath I might add, for approximately six hours about what you witnessed while living in the same home as the defendants. Isn't it true that the events you are describing were actually things that you, your brother and his crew did together?*"

Symone: "*No not at all.*"

Defense: *"Ms. Mitchell, can you please tell the courts why the defendants would have reason to believe that you were dead?"*

Everyone in the courtroom gasped and started talking loudly.

Judge: *"Order in the court! Order in the court!"*

Symone: *"They would think that because that's how we set it up to make sure I stayed safe until the trial. If they knew I was testifying against them they would've killed me."*

Defense: *"Who are we Ms. Mitchell?"*

Symone: *"Myself, and the detectives who handled this case."*

Defense: *"Isn't it true, Ms. Mitchell, that the real reason you told the detectives that it was my clients who did all of these things was because you needed to save yourself and your brother?"*

Symone: *"No. I'm just telling what really happened."*

Defense: *"Let's go through the events then, Ms. Mitchell. Who was it that set up the offices for the realty scam?"*

Symone: *"It was Jada that set them up."*

Defense: *"What if I told you that I had proof it was you and your brother, Ms. Mitchell, that set up all those offices in a fake name?"*

Symone: *"Well then your proof would be wrong because we didn't do that. We had nothing to do with it."*

Defense: *"Who was it that got all the furniture for the offices?"*

Symone: *"I don't know which one exactly, but one of them did."*

Defense: *"What if I said I also have proof that it was you and your brother who did that as well?"*

Symone: *"You would still be wrong. It never happened."*

Defense: *"Your Honor, I would like to play a recording of a message left by the witness on my clients' answering machine."*

Judge: *"Permission granted."*

As if on cue like the entire thing was planned to perfection, Pacatino's associate hit the play button.

Symone's voice on tape: *"Wass' up y'all this, Symone. I just wanted to tell y'all that my brother found somebody to rent the office and he gonna get the furniture too. So call me back and let me know what the deal is when y'all get this message."*

The entire courtroom began to talk loudly in response to what they just heard. The Judge banged his gavel again demanding order.

Defense: "*Ms. Mitchell, is that not you on that recording?*"

Symone stuttered.

Symone: "*I-i-it's m-e-e but...*"

Defense: "*Please just answer the question yes or no. Is that you on the recording?*"

Symone: "*Yes,*" she said putting her head down.

Defense: "*Your Honor, we'd like to enter this recording as evidence.*"

The Judge called out a number that the tape would go under.

The prosecutor looked all red and flushed in the face. He knew this cross was killing his most prized witness. Me and my girls sat with our legs folded and we each had a smirk on our faces. Pacatino continued.

Defense: "*Ms. Mitchell, this message was left before you and the girls lived together correct?*"

Symone: "*Yes.*"

Defense: "*Isn't it true that you never got a response back from that message you left because my clients had already told you they weren't interested in your little scheme?*"

Symone: "*No. It was their idea and they brought me in on it so they were interested.*"

Defense: "*Let us move on.*"

He looked over his notes and went through all the questions he had prepared for while she was on the stand testifying. He pointed out all the roles Symone played in the scams. By the time he got to the murders Symone was on the verge of tears but she held them in. This wasn't going according to the prosecution's plan at all.

Defense: "*Ms. Mitchell, I'd like you to take a look at this number and tell me if it belonged to you at one point.*"

He showed her a sheet of paper with a number written on it.

Symone: "*Yes, this is my old cell phone number.*"

Defense: "*Ok. You testified that there was a clean-up crew that handled the bodies after the murders took place. Isn't it true that these guys worked for you and your brother?*"

The jury and everyone else in the room got loud. They were shocked to see where this was going and it showed. The judge once again demanded order and advised that another outburst like that would cause him to clear the room.

Symone: *"No! Me and my brother didn't kill anybody."*

Defense: *"Ms. Mitchell, you, your brother and his crew killed these people for whatever reasons and when you all got caught by these detectives, you came up with this story, and worked out a deal with the detectives that you would be let off the hook if you testified! Is that not correct?*

State: *"Objection, Your honor! Speculation and the counselor is badgering the witness!"*

The Judge banged his gavel loudly trying to regain order in the courtroom. News reporters scurried out the room trying to get the story printed faster than the next. Finally the Judge was able to speak.

Judge: *"The objection is noted and sustained. Counselor you cannot submit such accusations without proof of the allegations. Unless you're prepared to support your claims, please refrain from making such allegations."*

Defense: *"Oh, the defense intends to prove it, Your Honor."*

Judge: *"I think it's been a pretty long day. Why don't we stop here and reconvene tomorrow morning at nine am."*

JADA

The trial was on every news station and in every newspaper by now. Reporters gave their ideas of how things were going and who it looked like was ahead. Some said the prosecution's case was extremely strong, while others reported that Pacatino was well ahead in the trial and if he continued then it was a strong possibility that we would be set free. Some reporters made comments about the chaos that was going on during the trial and all the allegations of the detectives being grimy and their key witness actually being the one who committed the crimes. They felt it would definitely be cause to declare a mistrial.

The following day when we got to court Pacatino and his team were in full force. It was time for the defense to make their case and he was more than ready. Although we didn't have as many witnesses to testify as the prosecution did, we were sure that the ones we did have, would be more than enough to get our point across.

My girls and I entered the courtroom with confidence. The media had been making comments about how beautiful we all were and how well we dressed during the trial. They said they've never seen a defense team so good looking. The radio stations made jokes about the difference in appearance when the cameras switched back and forth from the prosecution to the defense.

Everyone was settled and seated and finally Pacatino called his first witness.

Defense: *"We would like to call Cynthia Coto to the stand."*
A middle-aged woman stood up and walked over.
Defense: *"Ms. Coto, can you tell us where you work please?"*
Witness: *"I work for V-Com., a telephone company."*

Defense: *"And how long have you worked there?"*

Witness: *"I've been with the company since it started eleven years ago."*

Defense: *"And what is your title there at V-Com?"*

Witness: *"I'm the call center manager."*

Defense: *"Ms. Coto, do you remember the defendants from when they were employed with the company?"*

Witness: *"Yes, I do. They were lovely girls. I interviewed them myself when they were first hired."*

Defense: *"And could you tell the court, the shift the girls worked while they were under your management."*

Witness: *"They worked Monday through Friday from eight am to five pm."*

Defense: *"Are you sure about that?"*

Witness: *"Yes, I am certain. When you called me I had their files pulled by human resources."*

Defense: *"How long were the defendants employed with the company?"*

Witness: *"They were there for just under three years before they resigned."*

Defense: *"Ok Ms. Coto, I want to take you to the year 2002. Do you have the defendants file for that year?"*

Witness: *"Yes, I reviewed the file already."*

Defense: *"Great. During the months of September through March, in the year of 2002, how many times did the defendants call out of work?"*

Witness: *"They each called out three times during those months."*

Defense: *"What was the reason for those three call outs? Were they noted?"*

Witness: *"Yes, it was documented that one day they had dentist appointments, and the other two days were call outs due to inclement weather in December."*

Defense: *"Did they ever bring proof that they were at the dentist?"*

Witness: *"Yes, they each brought in documents from the dentist and we made copies and it was kept in their file."*

Defense: *"Ms. Coto, based on your experience as a manager, how would you rate the defendants work habits as far as how often they called out?"*

Witness: *"In my experience as their manager, I would have to say that they each had great work habits. They rarely called out and were always prompt and on time."*

Pacatino walked to the defense table and picked up a folder.

Defense: *"Your Honor, we would like to submit into evidence the file from my client's place of employment during the months in question with the realty claim."*

Judge: *"Does the prosecution have any objection to the file?"*

State: *"Yes, we do, Your Honor. Those records cannot indicate what the defendants did after the hours of five o'clock pm. They could've gone to those offices after work."*

Judge: *"Objection over ruled. This witness is not testifying that she knows what occurred after five pm. Her testimony clearly accounts for the defendants where abouts during the hours of eight am to five pm. I'll allow the file to be entered as evidence of that."*

The prosecutor sat back down looking defeated once again.

Defense: *"Thank you, Your Honor. No further questions for this witness."*

Judge: *"Would the prosecution like to cross?"*

State: *"One moment please, Your Honor."*

The prosecutor and his team whispered amongst themselves. They looked over their papers and whispered some more as if they were comparing the information they each held. The prosecutor slammed his folder down before replying.

State: *"No questions for this witness, Your Honor."*

Pacatino called two more witnesses that day. Two people that were victims of the realty scam. They told their told stories about what happened to them. Pacatino asked them both if they remember what day and time it was when they went to the office, one guy said it was on a Monday at about ten am and the lady said it was a Wednesday at about two thirty p.m. She said she was sure of the time because she left the office and went to pick her kids up from school directly afterwards. When they were asked if any one of us were at the office when they went there they both said no.

They said although it was a long time ago they were positive that it wasn't either of us.

Pacatino had both of them describe the person who helped them and they described a person with Symone's features. Angel quietly whispered to Lace that she remembered the guy on the stand.

"I could never forget those big ass glasses he had on because he still wearing them. When he was coming in the door I was just walking out to go get me and Symone something to eat and I remember laughing at his glasses in the car. So, Symone was there by herself when he got there."

Lace whispered what she said to me and we all quietly giggled.

On cross examination, the prosecutor tried his hardest to get the witnesses to say that it was a possibility that there were two people there and that they probably didn't remember. Or, the other person could have been in the rest room at the time. All his attempts were to no avail and the witnesses stuck to the fact that they only saw one person and it wasn't either one of us. There was nothing he could do with any of the witnesses and it wasn't a good luck for the prosecution.

We sat in the holding cell laughing and joking about how the trial was going.

"Oh it's funny now huh," Lace said to Angel. "A week ago ya ass was ready to cop a plea," she laughed.

"Fuck you, Lace! I was scared when that bitch got up there."

"Scared, ain't the word. Ya ass was ready to tell it all. Let me find out." I said.

"Whatever. You know it wasn't nothing like dat. I was just having a moment," she laughed.

"Ya punk ass gon' walk out the bathroom that day talking about you was gonna forget who I was. What did that mean, huh, Cleo? What it meant, killa?" I teased.

"It meant I ain't wanna go in ya mouth," laughed Lace.

"Yeah, whatever. Not if you like writing wit' ya hands you won't. Fuckin wit' me you gon' have to learn to write wit' ya toes you lift a hand to me, bitch," I joked.

We all laughed together not caring at the moment about the fact we were locked up. For a short while it felt like we were back home joking around in our living room. The only different was, we wasn't.

JADA

The following day Pacatino talked briefly with us while we waited for the judge to come in.

"Ok ladies, let's seal the deal today. We only have three witnesses left including those two clean up guys. Is there anything we left out? Anything else you think I should know?"

We all shook our heads no.

"Alright then."

"All rise!" said the bailiff as the judge came out.

Judge: "Please be seated. Is the defense ready?"

Defense: "Yes, Your Honor."

Judge: "Please call your witness."

Defense: "The defense would like to call Officer Jose Ramirez to the stand."

The short stocky officer stood up and made his way to the stand. He was sworn in and Pacatino wasted no time in questioning him.

Defense: "Officer, how long have you been on the police force?"

Officer Ramirez: "For five years now?"

Defense: "And for which district did you work back in 2005?"

Officer Ramirez: "During that time I was with the Philadelphia Police Department 7th District."

Defense: "And are you familiar with detectives Rogers and Wainwright from the 7th District?"

Officer Ramirez: "Yes I am."

Defense: "Officer Ramirez can you tell us about the conversation you over heard with the detectives regarding this case."

Officer Ramirez: *"Well...I was typing up a report when I heard them talking one day about it. Detective Rogers was saying to Wainwright that they couldn't make the arrest yet because they didn't have enough evidence."*

State: *"Objection, Your Honor! Hearsay!"*

Judge: *"Overruled. Please continue with your response."*

Officer Ramirez: *"They argued for a while about the evidence and Detective Wainwright made the comment that he didn't care about not having everything. He said they had enough to charge them and the rest they could buy."*

Defense: *"Did they say anything else?"*

Officer Ramirez: *"Yes Detective Wainwright was saying that he was up for a promotion if he could get the conviction and he wasn't letting anything stop that."*

Defense: *"Did you over hear anything about how they intended to get more evidence?"*

Officer Ramirez: *"Yes. I heard detective Rogers say that he could get a few people to come in and testify for the right price."*

Defense: *"And how did Wainwright respond to that?"*

Officer Ramirez: *"I heard him say that they could get the money from local drug dealers. He said all they had to do was catch a few of them with drugs and money on them and they could take the money, leave with the drugs and let 'em go. He said they wouldn't make any complaint's because they would be too happy that they weren't going to jail."*

State: *"Objection, Your Honor. This is all hearsay."*

Judge: *"Again, it's overruled. The witness is under oath testifying to what he heard being said counselor. It's admissible."*

The prosecutor threw up his hands and sat back down. He began whispering with his team again and writing stuff down.

Defense: *"Officer Ramirez, what did you think about you heard that day?"*

Officer Ramirez: *"Well, I figured no one would believe me there if I told. I had just been transferred to that unit and they always referred to me as the rookie who didn't know anything. They all had this thing of it being us against them meaning the cops against the criminals. They believed that no matter what you al-*

ways took care of each other, even if it meant lying and cheating the system a little."

Defense: "Did you believe the same?"

Officer Ramirez: "No, I didn't and I still don't. I believe in upholding the law and conducting myself as an officer who operates with honesty and integrity. I feel like if you wanna cheat the system then you're just as bad as the criminals?"

Defense: "And how were you treated by the two detectives because you wouldn't join in with the way they did things?"

Officer Ramirez: "They made it real hard for me there. They would talk our superiors into giving me bad assignments like traffic duty or security and things like that."

Defense: "Did a day come while you were on traffic duty that you saw the two detectives in the area you were working in?"

Officer Ramirez: "Yes."

Defense: "Can you tell us about that?"

Officer Ramirez: "Well, one day I was directing traffic in a very busy area not too far from here. I happened to see the two detectives pull up across the street from me. I was curious to know what they were up to because of all that I heard them say about this case. So I snuck up as close as possible to them without them realizing it. When I saw Detective Wainwright take out an envelope I immediately started taking pictures with my camera phone."

Defense: "And what did you do with those pictures?"

Officer Ramirez: "I downloaded them to my computer at home and then enhanced them to a better quality. That's when I saw the money sticking out of the envelope."

Defense: "And did you take the photos to your superior?"

Officer Ramirez: "Yes. I told him about the conversation I heard and let him know I thought that this could be one of the people they were paying to testify."

Defense: "And what were you told?"

Officer Ramirez: "He told me he would look into it but I should learn that I play for the home team and no one else."

Defense: "What did you think that meant?"

Officer Ramirez: "It meant that I needed to be quiet and not go against the detectives."

Defense: *"Officer Ramirez, can you tell us what you did after you saw that the information you gave your superior wasn't being looked into?"*

Officer Ramirez: *"I put in a request to be transferred from that district. I didn't want to be a part of such a corrupt unit."*

Defense: *"And were you transferred?"*

Officer Ramirez: *"Yes I have been a part of the 26th district since then."*

Defense: *"What did you do after you left that district?"*

Officer Ramirez: *"I waited until they made the arrest. When I found out who their lawyer was, I turned over the photographs...to you."*

Defense: *"Thank you no further questions, Your Honor."*

The prosecution then questioned Officer Ramirez about whether or not he knew for sure that's why the detectives were giving the guy the money. He said he didn't know for sure but he would bet his life on it that the reason was for him to testify. He was drilled and drilled by the prosecutor about being upset with the superiors at the 7th District for not giving him better assignments each day.

The prosecution argued that he was making up this story to get back at them for that. He continuously denied it and everything else that they threw at him he denied. When he stepped down from the stand he winked at us before walking out of the courtroom.

JADA

It was the last day for testimony. We couldn't wait to get it over with it so that we could find out the outcome. We were a little bit excited to find out who the clean up guys hired to take the fall and what they did with the bodies. So when the judge said for Pacatino to call their witness, we sat up straight and wide-eyed.

Defense: "The defense would like to call Bernard James to the stand."

The door that we came through opened and an officer escorted the guy out. He was dressed in an orange jump suit. The officer removed his handcuffs and he took his place on the stand. The news reporters and the jury all had confused looks on their faces. I know they were all thinking the same thing, *who the hell is this guy*?

Defense: "Mr. James, can you please tell the court why you're currently incarcerated?"

Witness: "I was convicted of murder a year ago," he responded in a tough tone.

Defense: "Is that conviction associated with this particular case in any way?"

Witness: "No it's not."

Defense: "How long were you sentenced too?"

Witness: "I got life. No parole."

Defense: "So it's safe to say that you don't stand to lose or gain anything by testifying today correct?"

Witness: "Yeah. That's correct."

Defense: "Mr. James, can you tell us how you made your living before you were arrested?"

Witness: *"I was what's known on the streets as a clean-up man."*

Defense: *"And can you describe what that means, please?"*

Witness: *"People would call me and my partner after they killed somebody and we would come and get the bodies and clean up the scene before the cops found out about the murder."*

Everyone in the courtroom gasped and began all talking at once loudly. They were shocked that the clean-up crew really existed and it showed. The judge restored order immediately.

Defense: *"Mr. James, can you tell us how you know the defendants?"*

Witness: *"That's the thing...I don't know them"* he said in his slow tough tone. He sounded a little bit like Brother man from the fifth floor that played on the T.V show Martin.

Defense: *"You don't know the defendants?"*

Witness: *"No sir, I don't know them, I mean all I know is they were friends of one our customers."*

Defense: *"And who is the customer that you're speaking of?"*

Witness: *"A girl name Symone."*

Defense: *"Would that be Symone Mitchell?"*

Witness: *"I never knew her last name. I just knew her by Symone."*

Defense: *"Ok. And how do you know Symone?"*

Witness: *"I told you, she was a customer."*

Defense: *"Can you describe for the court the work you did for Symone?"*

Witness: *"Well, she would call us up and tell us she needed us to come to different places after she killed somebody and we would go to where ever she said, clean up all the blood and anything else visible, and remove the bodies from the scene."*

Defense: *"Can you tell us how many times you received that call from Symone and how many clean ups you did for her?"*

Witness: *"It had to be like eight or nine jobs we did for her."*

The courtroom got loud again until the judge banged his gavel. The prosecutor called for an objection.

State: *"Your Honor, Symone Mitchell is not on trial here. The defendants are."*

Judge: *"Yes, I realize that. However, they are on trial for these murders and accused of disposing the bodies in a horrible manner. Objection over ruled."*

Pacatino asked the guy to describe all the jobs and locations that Symone called him to clean. He gave all the details of all of the murders.

Defense: *"Mr. James, were you told of the reasons the person that you were sent to clean up had been killed?"*

Witness: *"No. We never knew why. We didn't ask things like that and we were never told. We just did our job and that was it."*

Defense: *"Can you tell us where you took the bodies after you picked them up?"*

The girls sat up and listened.

Witness: *"My uncle had a funeral parlor. I had the keys to it. So we would take the bodies there and cremate them."*

The reporters went crazy. They jumped from their seats and ran out of the courtroom. This would be the biggest news update of their careers and they all wanted to be the first to release the information. The families of some of the missing people went crazy. They threw chairs, yelled screamed and cursed. The judge ordered them to be removed from the courtroom. Once it settled down Pacatino was able to continue.

Defense: *"Mr. James, can you tell us how you were paid for your services?"*

Witness: *"Symone would meet us after we did it. Sometimes the same day sometimes the next. But she paid us in cash. Ten-thousand dollars per job."*

Defense: *"Did she always contact you by phone when she needed a job done?"*

Witness: *"Yeah her cell phone. Always."*

Defense: And how did she reach you? Was it your cell phone she called?"*

Witness: *"Yeah, she called me on a number we only used for clean ups."*

Defense: *"Mr. James, do you remember what that number was that you had at the time?"*

Witness: *"Yeah. I remember it."*

Defense: *"And can you recite the number please?"*

He said the number and Mr. Pacatino wrote it on a sheet of paper. He read it back to make sure it was correct. He then went into his folder and pulled out a few sheet of papers that were stapled together.

Defense: *"Your Honor, I would like to submit into evidence a copy of Symone Mitchell's cell phone records from the years in question. It clearly shows the dates and times she called Mr. James' cell phone."*

He then showed the papers to the witness.

Defense: *"Mr. James, can you take a look at the highlighted number on these pages and tell me if that's the same number as the one you just gave?"*

He looked at all the pages.

Witness: *"Yes, it is my old number."*

State: *Objection, Your Honor...the defense cannot enter one of our witnesses' cell phones records as evidence. She is not the one on trial, sir."*

Defense: *"Your Honor, Symone Mitchell identified this number as belonging to her when she was on the stand. This phone record proves that she was the one making the calls to Mr. James to clean up the murders."*

Judge: *"Objection over ruled."*

Mr. Pacatino continued with his line of questioning.

Defense: *"Did she ever mention that her friends had committed the murder when she would call you?"*

Witness: *"No. She never said anything like that when she called."*

Defense: *"What would she say?"*

Witness: *"She would say stuff like, 'I got a mess on twenty Third Street', or 'I got another body I need handled.'"*

Defense: *"Would she specifically say I or did she ever use the word we?"*

Witness: *"She never said we. It was always the word I."*

Defense: *"Mr. James, are you sure you never seen or spoke to any one of the three defendants?"*

Witness: *"I'm positive. I would've tried to marry one of them they so fine."*

No one laughed at his joke. They still looked at him as a cold and heartless murderer. But his testimony definitely had their attention.

Defense: *"Thank you. No further questions."*

The prosecutor crossed examined the witness for thirty minutes before he finally gave up. Bernard wasn't changing his story and the theory that the prosecutor tried to pass off wasn't working with him. Mr. James even laughed at some of the questions he was asking. When he was done, it looked liked his cross hurt him more than it helped his case.

Pacatino called the last witness.

Defense: *"We'd like to call Anthony Johnson to the stand."*

Anthony came out the same door as the other guy also dressed in an orange jumper. Pacatino went through the same questions with him too. Not too much was different in his story except that Symone gave him a little more than money. He said he had sex with her twice but they never discussed the murders or the clean up. That was a rule he had. Never discuss business during pleasure. But he did say that she never mentioned to him that her friends killed any of the people they cleaned. He said that he always believed it was her and her brother and his crew who did it.

The prosecutor didn't attempt to cross seeing how bad the first one went. He believed he had made a strong enough case throughout the trial that it wouldn't make too much of a difference. The witness stepped down, was cuffed like his partner, and escorted through the door.

Defense: *"The defense rests, Your Honor."*

The judge looked at his watch. It was only twelve-fifteen.

Judge: *"I think we can take an hour for lunch then come back and do the closings if both sides are prepared?"*

State: *"Yes, Your Honor."*

Defense: *"That's fine."*

Judge: *"Okay, court is in recess for one hour. Please back by one-fifteen.*

During the lunch Pacatino and his team went over their closing remarks. They wanted to make sure they didn't miss a single thing.

We ate the food Pacatino had brought for us.

"I can't believe it's finally over," said Angel. "What y'all think gonna happen?"

"Man, I ain't worried about it. Pacatino did his thing, I bet we get off," said Lace.

"Well, you never know with these trials." I said. "I think he did the best he could under the circumstances, but now it's up to the jury."

"Yeah, I think the judge siding wit' Pacatino though," said Lace real confident. "You seen how he kept shuttin' dude down every time he tried to object to somethin'," she laughed.

"I know right. Too bad he ain't the one givin' the verdict," said Angel.

"Let's not even talk about it no more. I'm gettin' a lil nervous now," I said.

"Aiight then. So what you wanna talk about?" asked Lace.

"Anything, but the trial." I replied.

We rambled for the rest of the lunch hour just trying to keep our nerves down. It was getting closer for us to hear our fate and all three of us were more nervous that day than we had been during the whole trial.

When we got back from lunch, the prosecutor did his closing first. He reminded the jury about everyone that testified. About all the people that were scammed out of money and how they had been affected. He drove home the man from the credit card company and the video that showed a woman that looked like me. The guy who worked at the Best Buy store who said we bought lots of expensive things...*more* than the average person. He reminded them of the detectives who spent two years on the case and what they witnessed when they followed us around. He reminded them of Symone testifying that she was our roommate and saw first-hand what went on. He asked the jury to imagine the people that were killed being one of their family members. Finally, he said that we are beautiful in appearance and the jury should not be deceived by that. He said behind those beautiful faces, we were scam artists, vicious murderers and drug lords and we deserved to be put away for life for what they did.

When he was done, Pacatino stood up and took a deep breath. He began by reminding the jury that the testimonies of the prosecutors' witnesses were false. Some of them were paid to say what they said and the defense has proven that. He reminded them of the pictures of the detectives that were in evidence. He asked them to review Symone Mitchells' cell phone records that were submitted into evidence as well.

He reminded them of the officer who told about the things he heard them say and how they robbed the local drug dealers to get the money to pay for the false testimony. He reminded them of the lady who could not clearly ID his client because of the problems she had with her vision. He reminded them of the men hired to dispose of the bodies who stated that they never knew the defendants, only Symone Mitchell.

He constantly pointed out the fact that everything lead back to the prosecutor's key witness being the one who should be sitting before a jury, not his clients. He brought up the fact that there were no drugs found during the search or any counterfeit money or proof of credit cards being made by us. He said all that pointed back to Symone too. He finally ended by stating that they cannot return a guilty verdict unless there is not a single ounce of doubt in their minds that his clients are guilty of the charges. He stated that if there was even the slightest bit or any type of doubt in their minds, it is their duty and they are under instruction by the law to return a *not guilty* verdict.

Once both sides were done with their closing arguments, the judge gave the jury their instructions and turned over all the evidence to them from both sides. Our fate was now in their hands.

JADA

The courtroom was flooded with people when we got there. There wasn't an empty seat in sight. The media flooded the room waiting to hear the outcome. There were cameras everywhere. In the halls, more reporters were out there reporting that the verdict was in and discussing the details of the trial.

Me, Lace and Angel sat nervously in our seats along-side Pacatino. The jury had deliberated for four days about the case and it drove us crazy. When the Judge finally came out, you could hear a bird shit on cotton it was so quiet in there.

Judge: "Has the jury reached a verdict?"

A guy stood up and responded, "Yes we have, Your Honor." He passed the paper he was holding to the bailiff, who then handed it to the judge. He read the paper then passed it back.

Judge: "Will the defendants please rise."

We stood up and faced the jury.

Judge: "As to count 1 in the indictment, on the charge of conspiracy to commit fraud in real estate, how do you find?"

The guy on the jury read from his paper.

Jury Foreman: "As to the charge of conspiracy to commit fraud through real estate, count I of the indictment, we the jury, find the defendants NOT GUILTY."

Judge: "Was this decision unanimous?"

Jury Foreman: "Yes it was, Your Honor."

Judge: "How do you find on count II of the indictment?"

Jury Foreman: "As to count II of the indictment, on the charge of committing fraud through real estate, we the jury, find the defendants NOT GUILTY."

Judge: "Was this decision unanimous?"

Jury Foreman*: "Yes, Your Honor."*

Judge*: "How do you find on count III of the indictment, on the charge of conspiracy to commit fraud with the use of fake credit cards?"*

Jury Foreman*: "As to count III of the indictment, on the charge of conspiracy to commit fraud with the use of fake credit cards, we the jury, find the defendants NOT GUILTY."*

Judge*: "Was this decision unanimous?"*

Jury Foreman*: "Yes it was, Your Honor."*

We all gave Pacatino a hug as the foreman continued to call out not guilty on all the charges. When the foreman was done, the judge asked the foreman if the jury had anything further.

Jury Foreman*: "Yes, Your Honor, It is our belief, that all charges brought against these defendants, should be brought against Symone Mitchell and that she be tried in accordance with the law for the crimes committed. We further believe and instruct that the detectives from the 7th District Police Department that handled this case also be arrested and tried in accordance with the law and the allegations of corruption be investigated."*

The Judge thanked them all for their time and for doing their part in upholding our judicial system before he dismissed them. When he said the defendants were free to go, we continued to hug and thank Pacatino and his team. We all exited the courtroom together. Before we could even get into the hall good, reporters pushed cameras, microphones, and tape recorders in our faces and bombarded us with questions. Pacatino loved the limelight but me and my girls weren't feeling it. He escorted us to the car he had waiting outside and made sure we got in before he took any questions. He answered questions for about ten minutes before we finally pulled off.

We were locked up for ten months exactly. It felt good to be able to come and go as we pleased again. Zy had already taken care of our house and cars. When she went to see Rubin she had a moving company set up and prepare to move our stuff to Georgia. She didn't know what would happen to us but she followed the trial from beginning to end so she had a good feeling we would get off. When Pacatino passed me his cell phone, I was wondering who the hell it could be on the line.

"Hello." I said.

"Put the phone on speaker chick," said Zy.

I giggled and did like I was asked.

"Aiight. You on speaker," I said loudly.

"Heeyyy my, bitches!" yelled Zy through the phone.

We laughed and talked until we got to Pacatino's office building. He had a car there that he agreed to let us use for a few hours. We hung up with Zy, but not before promising that we would leave for Atlanta that night. She wanted to put us on the next flight out but I insisted that we drive. I said I had a few things to take care of first. I asked her to just reserve a truck for us and we would be fine.

"So where you put the money?" Asked Lace once we got in the car.

"I'm takin' y'all to it right now," I smiled.

"How you still not gon' tell us where you put it?" Angel said. "It's been damn near a year and you still wanna play this game," she laughed.

"Y'all gon see for your selves." I replied.

"I just hope the shit still there," said Lace.

"I told y'all it was safe, just chill. We got a nice lil ride ahead of us."

We drove for an hour and a half before I finally pulled in to a cemetery.

"What we doing here?" Asked Lace, sitting up in her seat.

"I wanna visit my parents before we go. I'll just be a minute," I said.

I got out the car and headed in the direction of my mother and father's crypt. While I walked, I thought about the people whose graves I had to walk over to get there. I thought to myself that I would never be buried in the ground like that. When my time came to leave this earth, I too, would be in the crypt with my parents. When I turned eighteen, I was given the only keys to access it. My aunt and uncle no longer had rights to enter the vault without my written authorization.

Once inside, I pulled the chair over to their coffins. I use to go and sit there for hours at a time. I talked aloud to my parents telling them how much I loved and missed them. I talked about my experience being locked up and going through that trial. When I spoke of the letter I received from Zy, tears fell as I apologized to my dad for Rubin. As much as I wanted to hate him for what he did, I knew it couldn't bring my mom and dad back. I told them that he was dying a slow death from cancer and that would be punishment enough for what he did.

Lace wanted to kill him but I refused. I said that would be the easy way out. I want him to suffer for all the years I suffered without my parents. I told them that I would be moving away but I would be there no matter what on Christmas, their birthdays, and the anniversary of their deaths every year. I wiped away my tears, kissed my fingers and placed it on their coffins.

I got up and walked down the small hallway. In the corner where one of the flowerpots laid, there was an opening behind the wall. I stood on the chair and reached down into the opening and pulled out three garbage bags. The money was safe just like I left it. I put the chair back and locked the crypt back up.

When I got back to the car, Lace and Angel were shocked to see the bags of money.

"Bitch, I thought you were just stopping to visit your parents," said Lace.

"Oh, I was. I just forgot to mention that I was gettin' the money too," I said with a huge smile on my face.

"I have to admit though, that's one hell of a hiding place, Jada," said Angel sitting in the back looking through the bags.

"I told y'all where I was puttin' it, nobody would find it."

"You damn sure were right," said Lace. "Let's get outta here. I'll drive."

We still had one more stop to make before we left P.A., I called Rubin to say I wanted to get all the stuff the guys put on the truck. I didn't want to see him at all so I was happy when the guy on the other end of the phone gave me an address to pick everything up. He said Rubin was unable to speak but he really wanted to see me. I said I would think about it and call back.

Pacatino had arranged for one of his associates to meet us at the car rental place so he could get his car back. Zy had reserved the only luxury truck they had on short notice, which was the 2010

Ford Explorer. We got the truck and headed for the address we were given.

When we pulled up, we looked around. The address we had turned out to be some sort of warehouse. We didn't see an entrance in the front, so we rode around the lot to the back where we saw a steel door. Lace banged on the door but got no response. I called Rubin's number back and told the guy we were outside the warehouse. A few minutes later, a real big fat guy opened the door and let us in. He took us to a room that was locked with a huge chain. Inside we found all of our stuff boxed up nice and neatly off in the corner. We looked inside the boxes to make sure everything was there. When we saw that it was, Lace asked the guy where the powder was. He pointed to a stack of bins. Lace walked over and checked the bins and it looked like all of it was there. Angel was over by the other boxes when she found our guns.

"Hey my pretty, little baby," she said to the gun like it was a real baby.

We all laughed and started to move the boxes and bins to the truck. The big guy stopped us and said he would take care of it. He and another guy loaded everything for us and we were out. We stopped for a bite to eat before getting on the highway to head to Atlanta.

JADA

The thirteen-hour drive from Philadelphia to Atlanta had us tired as hell when we got there. We all took turns driving to make it easier, but we still were tired by the time we got to Zy's house. It was a little after seven am when we pulled into the long driveway. We have only been there twice since Zy moved and almost forgot how beautiful the house was. When we got there, her mother had breakfast all ready for us which we were thankful for. We were hungry as hell. Jalen had gotten so big since we last saw him. He took us to his room and his playroom and showed all us his stuff like he always did when we got there. He would pull us from room to room saying, 'see this aunty' or 'look at that aunty.' He could barely talk the last time we were there so we thought it was so adorable.

We sat and got caught up wit' Zy and told her and her mother all about the trial and Symone being there.

"I still can't believe this bitch faked her death," said Zy. "So, she was in protective custody all this time?"

"Yup. That grimy bitch tried to get us locked up for life," said Lace. "It ain't over either. I know she gon' go in hiding being that we beat the trial. She gotta know we gon' handle her."

No sooner than Lace made the comment about Symone, did the trial come on the morning news. Zy's mother turned the volume up on the T.V and we watched.

The reporter was saying that Symone Mitchell was arrested just one day after the verdict in the trial of the Pennsylvania Queen Pins. He also said the 7th District Precinct was shut down temporarily and the lieutenant and several other officers and detectives were arrested on charges of corruption.

"I can't believe it!" Angel said.

"Shit, I can," said Lace. "If they wasn't tryna be so fuckin crooked then maybe we wouldn't be free right now. That's exactly what the fuck they get," she laughed.

"I'm mad they got to Symone before we did," I said.

"I know right. I had some nice things planned out for her," said Lace with an evil look on her face. "I hope she rot in that muthafucka for how she did us."

"Hell yeah," said Zy turning off the T.V. "I know y'all probably wanna take a shower and get some rest, so I'ma let y'all do y'all and when y'all wake up I got sumthin to show y'all."

"Dats Wass' up," said Lace. "Cuz I'm tired as hell."

We all got up and went to our rooms. Zy set up a room for each of us, when the movers delivered our stuff from the old house in P.A. She put all our stuff in the guesthouse. But when she heard the verdict, her and her mother spent the whole day setting up the rooms for us. The furniture and electronics were already set up in each room. We all unpacked our clothes, shoes, and accessories to make sure we were comfortable and didn't have to go through boxes to find our stuff.

———————————

It wasn't until the next morning that we all woke up. Sleeping in our own beds and not those hard bunk beds in the jail had us sleeping like babies. WE all got cleaned up and met up with Zy downstairs.

"Why you ain't wake me up?" I said.

"Girl, wake you up for what? I know y'all were tired and needed some rest, so I let y'all sleep."

"Yeah, but you said you wanted to show us somethin'," said Lace.

"It wasn't nuttin that couldn't wait until today. Y'all needed to sleep."

"So what you wanted to show us?" asked Angel.

Zy took us to the garage and opened it up. When we all saw our cars we screamed.

"Oh shit! I thought they took our shit," said Lace.

"Nope. I had them shipped when I went down there to meet Rubin."

"Damn, Zy. You really looked out," said Angel running her hand around the dust on her car.

"I tried to, girl. I prayed that y'all would beat that fuckin' trial everyday, I'm just happy y'all out. Anyway, enough wit' all dat. Let's get to the salon cuz I ain't never seen y'all hair look like it do now," she laughed.

"That's what I'm talking about!" I said. "I just need to drop this rental off and we can go."

We spent the whole day pampering ourselves. Hair, nails, pedicures, and shopping. When we were done, we looked like stars again. Zy was happy to have her girls back.

By our second week there we had already purchased some land and had the same builders who did Zy's house working on designs for our houses. We decided not to live together to give each other some space and privacy. Everybody was in agreement that it was time to let that part of our lives go. What we didn't know was what we were gon' do with the rest of the coke we had.

"So what you wanna do wit' the rest of the powder now that we out the game?" asked Lace.

"We gon do what we do," I responded. "Just cause we in ATL don't mean nuttin."

"So you wanna get rid of this and be done wit' it?" asked Lace.

"I don't know yet. We need to get rid of what we got now so it won't be in this house. After that we can figure out what we wanna do."

"I feel you," said Lace.

"I wonder what the market like out here," we all said in unison. We had to laugh at ourselves. Just then Zy walked in the room.

"What y'all plottin' on now?" she said in an, 'oh boy here we go again' tone.

"We ain't plottin'," I laughed.

"Yeah it's more like we tryna figure out what we wanna do wit' our lives you know," laughed Lace.

"Okay, and what did y'all decide?" asked Zy like she was afraid to hear the answer.

"We didn't," said Angel.

"But you know how we roll," said Lace. "It don't matter what we do, we gon get money. And anybody that try to stop us gon have a problem on their hands."

"I ain't gon tell y'all what to do. But no matter what I still got y'all back and I'ma ride for y'all," said Zy.

"So you back in?" I asked.

"I ain't say all dat damn," laughed Zy. "I'm just sayin."

We all laughed together knowin' damn well it was about put it down in the ATL.

At first glance all you would see was pretty girls who were beautiful and rich. What people who crossed our paths wouldn't know was that we were some scamming ass hustlers and murderers. And there was no telling what we would do next. Yeah, we were the unusual suspects. And anybody in our way, had betta watch out.

THE CARTEL street team

makin' this shit look too good...

Wanna earn some extra cash?
Join our street team and find out how?

Visit: www.thecartelpublications.com for more information.

The Cartel Collection
Established in January 2008
We're growing stronger by the month!!!
www.thecartelpublications.com

Cartel Publications Order Form
Inmates ONLY get novels for $10.00 per book!

Titles		*Fee*
Shyt List	_____	$15.00
Shyt List 2	_____	$15.00
Pitbulls In A Skirt	_____	$15.00
Pitbulls In A Skirt 2	_____	$15.00
Victoria's Secret	_____	$15.00
Poison	_____	$15.00
Poison 2	_____	$15.00
Hell Razor Honeys	_____	$15.00
Hell Razor Honeys 2	_____	$15.00
A Hustler's Son 2	_____	$15.00
Black And Ugly As Ever	_____	$15.00
Year of The Crack Mom	_____	$15.00
The Face That Launched a Thousand Bullets		
	_____	$15.00
The Unusual Suspects	_____	$15.00
Miss Wayne & The Queens of DC		
	_____	$15.00
Year of The Crack Mom	_____	$15.00
Familia Divided	_____	$15.00
Shyt List III	_____	$15.00
Raunchy	_____	$15.00
Reversed	_____	$15.00

Please add $2.00 per book for shipping and handling.
The Cartel Publications * P.O. Box 486 * Owings Mills * MD * 21117

Name: _____

Address:_____

City/State:_____

Contact # & Email:_____

*Please allow 5-7 business days for delivery. The Cartel is not
responsible for prison orders rejected.*